WHAT HE'S POISED TO DO

ALSO BY BEN GREENMAN

Superbad

Superworse

A Circle Is a Balloon and Compass Both

Correspondences

Please Step Back

WHAT HE'S POISED TO DO

Stories

BEN GREENMAN

HARPER ● PERENNIAL

NEW YORK ● LONDON ● TORONTO ● SYDNEY ● NEW DELHI ● AUCKLAND

HARPER ● PERENNIAL

The following stories have appeared, in slightly different form (and in some cases with different titles), in other venues: "What He's Poised to Do" in *The L;* "Barn" on Fivechapters.com; "The Hunter and the Hunted" in *OneStory;* "The Govindan Ananthanarayanan Academy for Moral and Ethical Practice and the Treatment of Sadness Resulting from the Misapplication of the Above" in *McSweeney's*, issue 29; "A Bunch of Blips" in *Lumina;* "To Kill the Pink" in *The Lifted Brow.*

In addition, the stories "What He's Poised to Do," "The Govindan Ananthanarayanan Academy for Moral and Ethical Practice and the Treatment of Sadness Resulting from the Misapplication of the Above," "From the Front," "Country Life Is the Only Life Worth Living; Country Love Is the Only Love Worth Giving," and "Hope" appeared in slightly different form in *Correspondences*, a limited-edition boxed set of stories published in 2008 by Hotel St. George Press.

HarperCollins books may be purchased for educational, business, or sales promotional use. For information please write: Special Markets Department, HarperCollins Publishers, 10 East 53rd Street, New York, NY 10022.

FIRST EDITION

Designed by Hotel St. George Press

Library of Congress Cataloging-in-Publication Data is available upon request.

ISBN 978-0-06-198740-3

10 11 12 13 14   OV/RRD   10 9 8 7 6 5 4 3 2 1

*To the people I've written to
and the people who have written back.*

"I'll write you a letter tomorrow
Tonight I can't hold a pen."
—PAUL WESTERBERG

CONTENTS

WHAT HE'S POISED TO DO

WHAT HE'S POISED TO DO

THE MAN IS NOT HAPPY AT HOME. WHEN HE SEES HIS WIFE OR his son, he knows that he should be, but he is not. The man is scheduled to take a trip from the city where he lives to the city where he sometimes does business. He packs a larger suitcase than is necessary. When he arrives in the city where he sometimes does business, he sends his wife a postcard that describes what little he understands of the problem, and how he intends to solve it—or at least begin to solve it—by not returning home right away. He knows he should not feel better after writing such a thing, but he does. He goes downstairs to the hotel bar. The bartender is a young woman. The man strikes up a conversation with this young woman, who has the same name as a woman he once dated. The man drinks until the young woman's shift is over, and then the young woman joins him for a drink at a corner table. A hand is placed upon a hand, and then upon a knee, and then between a knee and another knee. The young woman, in order not to notice, tells the man about her most recent love affair, and how she ended it by sending a postcard. The man laughs. He tells the young woman that they are the same kind of person. "You mean cowards?" she says. He removes his hand from between her legs. Now the young woman notices, and the man invites her upstairs, and she accepts, and they lean against one another in the elevator, and he undoes her skirt in the hallway, and removes it just inside his room. In the morning, she is not there, but she has left a postcard on his pillow beside him. He pieces together the previous night. He remembers that the woman called out his name, and that he laughed. He remembers that she took the phone off the hook theatrically. He remembers that she recited a series of dates for him: when she was born, when she was first married, when she had her son, who is almost exactly the same age as his son. His heart sinks. He does not like the fact that thinking of his son makes his heart sink. He takes a postcard from the desk and writes to his son. The man takes the postcard and puts it in the outer pocket of his suitcase, aware that he will never mail it. The next day, he does not see the young woman from the bar. He does not see her the day after that, either. He is busy with work, and when he is not working, he is walking up and down the city streets. He looks into the faces of the people he passes and tries to guess if they have ever betrayed someone they loved, or been betrayed by someone they loved. He supposes that most have, and this cheers him a bit, not for any reason other than the fact that it locates him. He returns to the hotel after the second day of working and walking and writes his wife a postcard. This one has a more optimistic message than the first: that, although he is not ready to talk on the telephone, he is ready to think about it, and that this is progress. He ends on a romantic note. He takes that postcard downstairs to mail it. The young woman from the bar is now working at the reservations desk. She pretends not to know him. At first, he is offended, and then he comes to understand that it is a game. She calls him sir, stiffly, and he hands her the postcard facedown, suddenly concerned that she might try to read it. She tells him that she would be happy to be of service. She calls him sir again, with no additional warmth. He returns to his room. An hour later, there is a knock at his door. He opens it to find the young woman there. This time, she undoes her skirt herself. The next morning, he remembers that she did not call out his name, but that she looked at him as if she was thinking of doing so. He remembers that she recited a series of names: her father's name, her husband's name, her son's name. He is surprised to find that it is the same as his son's name. He keeps this information to himself. The next morning, there is another postcard from her next to him on the bed. He hears the shower. He hurries and writes a postcard in response and places it on the pillow next to the one that she has written. She returns to the bed, not completely dry, and the water from her skin smudges the ink of the postcard he has written in response. She speaks to him in the same stiffly formal voice she used downstairs, at the desk. She calls him sir rather than using his name. She lists for him all the things she has done for him, and all the things that she plans to do. She leaves him sleeping, this time, without a postcard. Two more days pass. He does not see the young woman. He speaks to his wife once on the phone. She cries, softly at first and then in gasping sobs. He explains that this is why he didn't want to talk on the telephone. She asks him when he's coming home. He says that he has one more day of work and then he will decide. Her tone hardens and she tells him to be sure to let her know. When she hangs up, he is seized by the desire to write her another postcard. Instead, he writes one to his son. This one also goes into the zipper pocket of his suitcase. He goes downstairs to get a drink. The young woman is not in the bar. He asks the bartender, who says that he thinks she's on the reservations desk. He goes to the reservations desk. There is another woman there, who says that she thinks the young woman is working in the bar. He sits in a chair in the lobby, feeling lost. He reads a newspaper and a magazine, retaining nothing, not even the pictures. Out of the corner of his eye, he sees a young boy. The boy looks faintly like his son and then, as he comes closer, more and more like him. The resemblance is uncanny: the face is the same shape, the hair is the same color, the eyes shine the same way. The man hears a woman's voice calling the young boy. It is the young woman from the bar. The woman sees him and approaches. She introduces her son. The man shakes the boy's hand with exaggerated formality. The boy laughs. He even laughs like the man's son. The man does not tell the young woman how much her son resembles his son. Who would that benefit? The young woman tells the man that she will be working reservations later that evening. She says that at the end of her shift, she will be happy to come upstairs to pick up any mail he has to send. Her tone is falsely playful. The man goes for a walk. He looks into the faces of the people he passes, but this time he does not try to guess anything. He returns to his hotel room and undresses. He runs the shower but does not step into it. He stretches out on the bed. He feels his excitement growing as he anticipates the young woman's visit. He thinks that maybe he should greet her at the door with a postcard that lists all the things he expects her to do for him, or all the things he has done. He also thinks that he owes his wife another call, or at least another postcard. He turns on the television. There is a boy on the television who does not look anything like his son. He sits down at the desk, finds a pen, and holds it over a postcard, uncertain exactly what he's poised to do.

HOPE

TOMAS TINTA WAS BORN IN THE CITY OF CAMAGÜEY IN CUBA on the ninth day of April in the year 1923. He was the son of a hardworking Spaniard named Antonio Tinta, who was the proprietor of a shoe store in Camagüey. Tomas's mother, Camilla Garcia, also hailed from Spain, where she had been considered a great beauty. Comfort and love filled the Tintas' Camagüey home, which was completed by the addition of a baby girl named Sofia in 1926; the Tintas basked in the glow of their mutual love for their children and their success as entrepreneurs, which led them to open three more shoe stores. But then, in 1935, suddenly and without warning, Antonio Tinta was called back to eternity, and all at once things changed. The money that Antonio had earned from his first stores had, the family discovered, gone into opening the later stores, and Camilla, try as she might, could not make sense of the business. Two years after Antonio went into the ground, his beloved wife followed. Sofia went to stay with a cousin in Havana, an elderly devout who believed she could raise girls up into proper women. She did not have the same confidence when it came to boys, and so Tomas was placed in the care of a friend of the family, a country doctor named Ferrer. Dr. Ferrer was of high standing but not of high character. He beat Tomas when he did not listen to him or when he looked at him. Tomas endured a life of great privation and violence. Five years after coming to Dr. Ferrer, Tomas was finally able to rejoice when the doctor followed his dear parents down into the hereafter.

By this time Tomas was old enough to enter a trade school, and so he did. He began training to become a typesetter. As luck would have it, a distant cousin of his mother was a head operator at a company in Havana. The city was a tonic. Work kept his mind sharp, and he was reunited with his sister, Sofia, which brought him much joy. Pleased with his apprenticeship at the printing company, Tomas set his sights on becoming a full type operator, and as the law required an age of sixteen, he falsified documents to that effect. He was a printer, after all. He was awarded his certification.

In the early part of 1940, an event occurred that changed Tomas Tinta's life forever. It took place on the last day of March, when Tomas, in search of work in Havana's type shops, met a woman named Yamila Rodriguez. Tomas had a coffee in his hand and spilled it when he saw her. "My hand went limp with fear and hope," he wrote to her in a letter that was composed on the first day of April. "The apparition had jet-black hair and a ripe little plum of a smile. I could not tell whether she was smiling at me or past me, and then I came to realize that they were one and the same, because I had been expanded by that smile." This is the first known letter written by Tomas Tinta; it is also the first of more than two thousand letters he wrote to Yamila Rodriguez. In the second letter, written the very next day, Tomas confessed his unconditional love for her. "A man who has discovered love in his heart can pretend to wait before making his declaration," he wrote. "But that would be like visiting a museum, standing before a masterpiece, and reserving judgment. What would be the point, apart from stubbornness and pride?" According to a letter of April 19, Tomas had revealed his new love for Rodriguez to his sister, who took the news with cautious enthusiasm. "She told me that she had always felt that my heart was a fragile vessel, and as such it should not be filled too quickly for fear of shattering it. I assured her that my feelings have quite the opposite effect, and that they are giving me a strength I could not have imagined. She then asked if she could meet you, and I told her that if she has met me, she has met you, so tightly woven together are our souls. This answer did not satisfy her. Perhaps you can come for dinner one day soon."

It is not known whether Rodriguez ate dinner with Tomas and Sofia. What is known is that, in early May, she disappeared from Havana entirely. Tomas continued to write letters regularly, and these letters remained passionate and poignant. They were not, of course, mailed, as he did not know her whereabouts. On the first of July, Tomas boarded the ship *Leandro* and sailed for Miami, Florida. "I do believe I know where you are, my Yamila," he wrote in a letter during the voyage, "or rather, I believe I know where you are in addition to being in my heart. It is said that a man cannot spend his entire life in pursuit of one goal, particularly if that goal is merely a woman. Merely a woman? This strikes me as a terrific affront. Better to say 'merely a cathedral' or 'merely a gold mine.'"

Arriving in Miami, Tomas could not find a station in his given career, so he took work as a clerk in a shoe store, which was a bittersweet reminder of his youth. He continued to write to Rodriguez at a steady rate but did not mail his letters, as her location was still a mystery. The correspondence only occasionally reveals disappointment or frustration in Tomas's tone. More typical is a February 1941 letter that reads, in part, "Today I spent some time by the water, walking along it, gazing across it, wondering which of these behaviors, each of which a mathematician would correctly call a 'vector,' most accurately reflects my position with regard to you. Am I walking alongside you, always, or looking across an expanse to find you?"

In the spring of that year, Tomas was badly injured in an automobile accident. For one month both of his arms were in a cast; this is one of only two sustained gaps in his ongoing correspondence with Rodriguez. When Tomas resumed his letter-writing, in mid-May, he once again did so with a regularity that did not ebb even when, in June, he struck up an intimate relationship with a daughter of the city of Miami named Eileen Ogham. The relationship had no discernible effect on the correspondence; in fact, Tomas even wrote freely to Rodriguez about Ogham. "Eileen and I are traveling up to Sarasota tomorrow, where she has an uncle. I think she expects me to romance her in the most obvious manner." Tomas did so, evidently, because in July he wrote to Rodriguez that he and Ogham were to be wed. "I love her," he wrote, "and I will tell you all about it when I see you, my dear Yamila. The two of us, entwined from the start of time and still in that most exalted of states, will sit at the shore and watch the waves recede like all that we have forgotten: I mean not that the waves will go away like the events that we have forgotten, but that they will go away like forgetting itself."

At the shoe store, Tomas befriended several customers, including some soldiers. One of them had been a newspaper reporter before the war, and when he returned to his position after the war's end, he recommended Tomas to a position as a typesetting foreman. He began his employ on the sixth of March of 1947.

Three months later he and Eileen had their first child, a daughter named Julia. "She was a light to me from her first moments, just as you were," he wrote in another unmailed letter to Rodriguez. "Do you remember how I felt when I first saw you on that Havana afternoon? Perhaps you cannot, and neither can my daughter. I held her in my arms and felt the rapid beat of my heart." A second child, a boy, followed. "Thomas is his name," he wrote to Rodriguez. "He is a scamp compared to Julia, who is something of an angel. I have spent some time imagining how they will look when they are older. Thomas, I think, has Eileen's features. Julia has, I like to imagine, my sister's. I imagine that you are curious to learn more about Sofia. In that, again, we are one. She has not written or called me since I left Cuba. I wonder if she is well."

In 1949 Tomas lost his printing job and was forced to return to the shoe store, and the amount he was able to earn there was not enough to keep food on the table. Then the store suffered a small fire and Tomas was forced to take work as a busboy in a café, where the pay was worse still. "At least I can bring home food at the end of the day for my wife and children," he wrote to Rodriguez. "Yesterday I was packing up the food, which consisted primarily of burned meatloaf that could not be served, and I found myself thinking of you. Inexplicable, perhaps, but the thought was strong and sudden and brought a blush to my face. I will tell you about it soon. Now, I have limited time. I am going to meet with Eileen's father. In my time of trouble, her parents have not offered any help and in fact they have turned against us in a surprising way." The meeting seemed successful. But this was an illusory success; before the end of the year, Eileen had left Tomas to take up with another man. "It is painful," Tomas wrote to Rodriguez, "to imagine him raising my children as his own."

Tomas passed through a period of extreme exhaustion, though

he was still a young man. "I am passing through a period of extreme exhaustion, though I am still a young man," he wrote to Rodriguez. He took as a girlfriend the daughter of a man who owned a diner. For a year, insensible to all but the most basic needs, he lived with this new woman, Anna, as man and wife. "Even though she is only nineteen," he wrote to Rodriguez, "she is wise, and she has recently been telling me that I need to try to have my family again. I think she has no other reason to say so except her goodness, which was an idea I had stopped believing in, and was on the verge of killing in myself. I have even been thinking of stronger evils like robbery."

"Yes, robbery," he wrote to Rodriguez the next evening. "I know when the office is left unattended and where the keys are kept. I will never act upon it, because I am an honest man, and in my honesty I grow more and more certain of nothing except my sadness. And yet, there are glimmers of hope in this bleakness. I should have mentioned them yesterday. One night, in the dim days before Anna told me that I had to get back to my family, I slept outside in the street, dizzy and miserable, and I considered ending my life. Instead, I started to talk to a man who came to the restaurant who owned a cigar store. He knew a man who owned a cigar factory, and when I told him I was from Camagüey, I was hired immediately. There was a job that required setting type for the labels for the cigar boxes, and here my Spanish was useful. My boss at the factory is a terrible man named James Hooper who reminds me in every way of Dr. Ferrer, and I turn my head when I go by him for fear of being hit. Still, it is work, and work gives a man pride and money, and money is only dirty when you do not have any of it at all, and the little bit I am making these days is cleansing me somewhat, to the point where I can once again recognize myself in the mirror."

He continued the following day. "My next step is to make contact with Eileen. I will let you know how it goes, my Yamila."
Three days later he resumed: "I made contact last night. It was
raining. I stood under an awning. When I saw her coming, I
stepped out into the rain, partly so that she would not pass by
and partly so that she would not see the tears on my face. She
cried, too. She told me that my daughter was missing me every
day and that the man who had been with them was gone now. She
said that she loved me still, but she also said that she did not have
trust for me any longer. She asked me to go away."

Another month passed over the planet, during which time
Tomas did not write to Rodriguez. This is the second and last
known gap in the correspondence. Among Tomas's papers, there
are a number of false starts: "Dear Yamila, I have long wondered,"
began one. "It is morning," read another. "It is evening," another.
Then, one day, he took up pen and composed another letter. "I
will tell you, Yamila, that when I finally saw Eileen again it was
a sunny day," he wrote. "I asked her to go with me to sit in the
park. She agreed. It was almost sundown and we sat there next
to one another. Between us there was an invisible wire and I
followed it first with my eyes and then with my hand, which I
placed gently on her knee. She laughed. I took back my hand. She
said that no, a hand on her knee in the grass was exactly what
she dreamed about. She took my hand in hers then. We sat in the
grass. I placed my head on her bosom as if I were a child and she
were the earth, and I clung to her for my safety as I often dream
of clinging to you."

The next letter was dated two days later. "My dearest Yamila,
I make it a practice to eat once each week at the diner that Anna's
father owns. I see her there sometimes, and though she is with
another man now, though she is carrying his child, she is still

close to me in ways I cannot explain to my satisfaction. When I went there last week, she asked me why I seemed happy and I told her, as best as I am able; the words fill my heart but cannot always make the journey to my mouth. 'You have hope,' she said, and I agreed, saying 'yes' and then saying nothing. I have hope, but I am unsure whether I am to act on it or not. If I act, there is the possibility of gain but a greater possibility of loss. The sweetness of hope will last only until I take action, at which point it will vanish. I force my mind to realize this. Is hope a spiritual state? I carry out this petition in hope's name. And so I remain in the grass with Eileen, sitting there, touching her hand. I remain with you in the café in Havana, watching your hand round off a sentence in the air. I remain with my sister, reunited for the first time. I remain with my poor dear mother, at her bedside. That is a continual paradise. And yet, I am still rooted to the earth. I am still a poor man. I am still the son of two parents who are in the ground. I am still at the cigar factory, still a slave of James Hooper, whom I turn away from each time I pass him by. Yamila, my darling, my love, I will write you tomorrow, and the day after that, and every day on into eternity." He did.

BARN

SHE'S OLDER. THAT'S THE FIRST THING YOU NEED TO KNOW about her.

I'm pregnant. That's the first thing you need to know about me.

Our favorite colors are one color, blue. Even two sisters who are very different can be similar. You should know that, too, because it may explain the way things went.

I MARRIED A FARMER. I didn't plan to do it. It just happened. To be fair, I didn't know he was a farmer. He was just a guy I met at a dance, and then later he came into the hardware store where I was working and pretended to be surprised to see me. We went out on two dates before I even got his name right—I thought it was Bert and it turned out to be Berne, which is such a strange first name that I don't think I can be blamed for my mistake. My sister's husband, Ed, who owned the hardware store, said that when he first saw the name on a personal check he thought it was Verne, and he blinked twice to get the B to turn. But it didn't. It was Berne. Berne never had trouble with my name. Who has trouble with Susan?

Berne and I dated for eleven months. He bought me presents all the time: a necklace with a heart-shaped charm, a red scarf, a hat. Then we broke it off when I went to McCook Community College to learn to be a medical secretary. My parents wanted me to go. My mother, in particular, was sold on the idea. She told me that a marriage was one thing, but you always needed a career.

We wrote to each other. He wrote more often, and though he was unpracticed at it—he spelled about every third word wrong, and his punctuation was a form of improvisation—it made me love him more, because I saw how I could improve matters. I used to tell friends at McCook that I had a boy waiting for me at home. They would nod or smile and I'd complete the thought; "He's waiting to become a man," I'd say.

Then we broke it off. That's what I like to say, but really he broke up with me because he thought I was dating my teacher, Mr. Carr. This wasn't true at all, of course. Once Mr. Carr and I went out to coffee because he said he needed to talk to me about my exam, but after about fifteen minutes it became painfully clear that he had nothing at all to say about the exam, and that he just wanted to tell me all about his divorce, and how his wife couldn't give him any kids. I guess I felt sorry for him, because I went back to his house after that, but we didn't do anything except sit around on the couch with the outsides of our legs touching each other. Then he leaned over and kissed my shoulder. His lips were cool on my skin. I didn't tell him to stop, but I didn't encourage him and I left a few minutes later.

I don't even know how Berne found out. Maybe I mentioned it because it seemed like such a nothing. But it wasn't nothing to Berne—he lowered his voice almost to a whisper, which was far worse than yelling. I went out with Mr. Carr only once after that, and then just to tell him that even though I respected him as a teacher (which wasn't really true) and liked him as a person (which wasn't really true either) I couldn't see him anymore because I had a guy back home who wanted to get more serious. This time I didn't say a boy, and that was true, and before I knew it, I was Mrs. Berne Moser, and I was throwing the bouquet over my shoulder. It stayed in the air for a while, and then Sarah caught it.

How can it be that my sister was in line to catch the bouquet when she had a husband who owned the local hardware store? Easy. He died. ED MCCAFFREY, 58, OWNED MCCAFFREY'S HARD-WARE. That was the headline in the paper. Ed was a rough-and-tumble guy, always getting into a scrap over the silliest thing. Once he threw another guy through a window because the guy didn't like *Some Came Running*, which was Ed's favorite movie of all time. Sarah was always worried that Ed would die in a bar fight or in a motorcycle wreck. But neither of those things happened. He died of a sudden heart attack, behind the counter at the hardware store. It was the counter where I worked for hundreds of days, but when I went back there after Ed's funeral, it didn't seem like the same counter at all. It was still and quiet, with none of the glorious mess. The register drawer was open, which it never was, and it was empty, which it never was. One of the other clerks said that they buried Ed with his money, but I wasn't sure whether that was a kind of knock on Ed for being a notorious cheapskate or a kind of joke about how much he loved his business, so I didn't say anything.

*   *   *

ED HAD A SON from his first marriage, Dave. Ed always said that it was in honor of his uncle Dave, and not Frank Sinatra's character in *Some Came Running*. Sarah always said that she never met Uncle Dave and didn't think he existed. Dave worked in the hardware store with me when I first started there. I was nineteen and he was seventeen. Ed wasn't my brother-in-law yet, just my boss. So Dave was nothing to me, until he was something. We locked up late sometimes, and one time he told me that I was looking pretty, and the next thing you know we were crouching down under the key counter, kissing. Every time he moved or I moved the whole thing jingled like Christmas, so he tried to stay still and so did I. We saw each other a few times after that, and then I started going with this older guy and Dave kind of got his feelings hurt. The older guy wasn't Berne, not yet. Berne was two guys later, and by then Dave had quit the hardware store and gone to Lincoln to try to be a painter. Not a house painter or a sign painter, either. A real painter. Ed always joked about how any man who painted was a fruit, but I know that he was proud of Dave because he hung his paintings in the back office of the hardware store. One of them was of a woman standing by a window, looking out. She was real pretty and had a faraway look in her eyes, but faraway like she was thinking about something in her past rather than in her future. Dave told me that it was a girl who posed for him in Lincoln. He also told me that she was the second girl that he ever kissed, and that she wasn't as good as the first. Go on, I said. Flattery will get you nowhere. I didn't tell Sarah about the woman in the painting, but we both agreed it was a nice painting because it was mostly blue.

*   *   *

DAVE WAS ALWAYS REAL CLOSE to his dad. They drank together almost every day, from when Dave was just a boy until Dave left town. Ed wasn't one to keep a boy from drinking. "Thirteen," he said, like that was an explanation. When Sarah married Ed, she told me that she and Dave didn't get along, not because Dave couldn't accept her as his stepmother but because he couldn't accept having less of his father's attention. Sarah liked talking that way; when she was at McCook, she took one psychology class, and she wore it proudly whenever she could. I told her that it would get better, that Dave was a nice guy who didn't usually hold a grudge over stupid things.

I was wrong. Dave didn't like her to start with, and after about six months the two of them hated each other. He called me once when he was back in town and said he didn't understand how I could be sisters with such a stuck-up, dull, foolish kind of person. I told him that Sarah and I were different, but not so different. He told me that I needed to think more highly of myself. Then he started telling me that I was still on his mind. While he was talking, Berne walked in the room, and I had to pretend it was the grocer on the phone so that Berne wouldn't get suspicious.

BERNE'S DAD WAS A FARMER, but he was also a banker. He gave loans to other farmers. Berne has shown me pictures of his father when he first came to town in the thirties. He was a nicely dressed man, as handsome as his son, and he was always smiling. In the pictures, at least. To hear Berne tell it, he took a turn for the worse after he married Berne's mother, who was the kind of woman who liked to tell her husband one thing and do another thing. That other thing, mostly, was running around with other men. Berne said that was the main reason he was so jealous, because his mama made a fool of his daddy. The men in town who were friends of Berne's daddy used to tell him to leave. Ed wasn't one of those men—he was a roughneck, and Berne's daddy was a gentle soul—but he was a man people listened to. You know, he liked to say, if I had a woman like that, it would put crazy thoughts in my head.

Berne's daddy had a saying in return: when a man has crazy thoughts in his head, he should count to ten and pray that those thoughts go away. Ed and Berne's daddy must have been talking about two different kinds of crazy thoughts, because at some point Berne's daddy couldn't count to ten anymore. Instead, he went out to the barn, looped a rope over the main beam, and hanged himself until he was dead.

WHEN BERNE'S DADDY DIED out in the barn, Berne buckled down. He became more himself, more careful, more quiet. When Ed died of his heart attack, Dave went to seed. He wasn't even going to come back for the funeral, he told me on the telephone, because coming back was proof that his dad was dead. I told him that he needed to pay his respects, and that he needed to think about Sarah for a minute, also, because she loved Ed as much as Dave did, and this was a time when they needed to set aside their differences. He didn't say anything on the telephone, but he must have liked my advice because the morning of the funeral he showed up at the church, clean-shaven, eyes bright, mouth set in a serious line. I'm just going to stay for the day, he told me, but he was in town the next day, and the day after that, and after a month it became obvious that he wasn't going to make it out of town any time soon, and that the line of his mouth wasn't going to stay so straight. Mainly it was the drink, although the women didn't help either. He set up a studio over the hardware store and started painting all the girls in town. Some of the fathers of the girls weren't too thrilled about having a young painter like that set up shop in their midst. It was probably one of those fathers who went by Dave's studio one night and beat him up. He was in pretty bad shape afterward, not because the beating was so severe but because he slipped down the stairs while he was leaving his studio and ended up smacking his hipbone on the banister-post.

I let him come live in the barn of Berne's farm. Berne wasn't too pleased about the arrangement, but not because he suspected anything about me and Dave. He wasn't too pleased because it was so soon after the wedding, and he wanted to have some time for the two of us, and also because he's just that type of guy: not too pleased. I told him that I felt responsible for Dave because he was kind of my nephew, being my sister's husband's son. "We're all knots on the same rope," I told him, and I don't know if he liked the sound of it or not, but he nodded. I also reminded him how hard it was for him to lose his own father, and that Dave wasn't as strong a person inside. And then I told him that if he let Dave come to stay with us, I would be a very good wife, if he knew what I meant, and he did, and he rolled his eyes and laughed. "If you're not trying to make babies, Susan, it's a sin," he said.

IT WAS BECAUSE OF BERNE'S FATHER THAT, when we were dating, half the time he said he didn't want any children. Children just keep people together who shouldn't be together, he said. The other half of the time he said he wanted children because children are the best part of love. "Not sex?" I said. I was just joking, of course, but he got all serious. "I have two rules," he said. "One is to honor and love, and the other is to keep procreation sacred."

I have only one rule, and that's that I refuse to have only one child. Only children like Berne and Dave end up with this idea that everything their parents do is because of them. Children with brothers and sisters, like me and Sarah, have it better. We learn to talk, to joke, to watch as power shifts, to spare the feelings of others, to wait and see.

There are many examples, but I can only think of one now. When I was about eight, and Sarah was about ten, our daddy lost his job in the post office. For about six weeks, he was at home, and he was driving everybody crazy, rearranging the items in the kitchen, polishing things he'd never looked at before, let alone polished. The main thing he did was ask us to play catch in the yard. Every hour of every day it seemed like he wanted to play catch: to go outside and toss a tennis ball back and forth. He said it soothed him. For some funny reason, he wanted only one of us out there at a time. Probably because it doubled the amount of time he could spend playing catch. One day, Sarah was out there for about an hour, and then she ran in and took a popsicle out of the freezer. "I'm not going back out," she said. "You go." She sat there sucking on the popsicle, and when I asked her if that was more important than our daddy's feelings, she shrugged. "It's hot out there," she said. "And I can't make him feel better. He thinks I can, but I can't."

I didn't want to go outside either, so I didn't. After about twenty minutes, our daddy still hadn't come inside, and my mom told me I had better go out and see what was keeping Frank. She always called him Frank, even to me. I went to the yard and found him sitting on the back stairs, bouncing the tennis ball between his knees. "You ready?" he said.

I shook my head. "Just coming to see what's keeping you."

"God damn," he said, and threw the ball over the back fence, as far as it could go.

SARAH AND I WERE CLOSE. She was only two years older, which meant that all the things that happened to me were fresh in her memory. Getting your period, kissing, going to second base, but also other stuff, like how to dress on your first day in school, and how to hold a cigarette so that you didn't look like you were imitating someone from the movies. She was always a little louder than me and a little wilder. When she was sixteen, she was going with this boy and she got pregnant, and she had one of her friends drive her down south of Lincoln for an abortion. She made me promise not to tell our mom or dad, and I didn't. After that she was afraid that she couldn't get pregnant again, and maybe she was right, because she didn't from the next guy, whom she went with for two years, and she didn't with the guy after that, whom she lived with for a year, and she didn't with Ed. Right at the beginning of her time with Ed, our dad died when he had a stroke while driving, and for a few weeks we talked every day on the telephone. Our mother was sick by then, too, with lung cancer, and she was in and out of the hospital. I hope she goes soon, Sarah said. She needs to be with Frank. That was the other thing about only children: when parents passed, there was no one who felt the same exact things you were feeling.

WHEN DAVE CAME TO LIVE in the barn, he told me he was going to start a new life. "No more drinking," he said, "and no more girls."

"Good," I said. "We can begin our new lives together." He broke both rules the first week—I saw a small box of empty bottles stacked against the wall, and once I knocked on the barn door and heard noise inside, but no one answered.

When I asked him about it, he denied that there were any girls. "I told you," he said. "I have a new life now." He was propped up on pillows on a narrow board he used as his bed, sketching with a piece of charcoal.

"What are you drawing?" I said.

"Pictures of the things I can't do anymore," he said.

I didn't care what kind of rules he broke. What did I care? Berne was less generous. He grumbled about Dave: Why would we let a man like that into our home, especially when we were trying to begin our own life together? I could see him getting angrier and angrier, but it wasn't like Berne to do anything other than grumble. Finally, he asked me flat-out if there had ever been anything between me and Dave, and I said absolutely not, and he asked me if I was telling him the truth, and I just stared at him like he was crazy.

Sarah asked me why I didn't tell Berne the truth. "Because he wouldn't understand," I said.

"I guess not," she said. "Who would understand that a nice girl like you ever had a thing for that dirty little drunk?"

"Are you still thinking of moving?" I asked Sarah. Ever since she caught the bouquet she'd been telling me she needed to get out of town. On weekends she went to Lincoln; she was seeing a guy there sometimes.

"I don't know," she said. "This town isn't doing much for me. I have a little money from selling the hardware store. I am seriously thinking about getting out of here."

"Would you go to Lincoln?" I said.

"I don't know," she said again. "The problem with this guy is that he wants a family."

"Don't you want kids?"

"If I can have them."

"You can."

"Are you a doctor?" she said.

"Yes," I said.

FOR A LONG TIME, Berne and I weren't getting pregnant either. He thought it made me sad, and he bought me lots of presents: another necklace (this one had a cross), another scarf (this one was blue), another hat (it looked just like the first). I didn't like the necklace or the hat, but I loved the scarf. I wore it all the time, and even Sarah agreed that it looked like a dream on me. But then I lost it. Berne never seemed to notice, and I certainly didn't mention it. Then I got pregnant, and it didn't seem to matter anymore. Berne told me that the baby was a girl, that he was sure of it.

"I want to name her Laurel," he said, "after my father's mother. If it's a boy, I don't have any ideas."

ONE DAY IN WINTER, I was out in town, getting some things for the house, and I came home to find a note from Dave on the counter: it was folded up and tucked inside an envelope, though the envelope wasn't sealed. It said he couldn't stay anymore. It thanked me for my generosity. It told me that we would always be special to each other, even without Ed, even without the hardware store. It said that there was a painting in the barn for me, the portrait of the woman that Sarah and I liked so much. It didn't mention Berne.

I went out to the barn. Even before I got there, I knew that there was someone inside. "Dave," I said. "What's with this note?"

But it wasn't Dave. It was Berne. He was standing over Dave's bed, looking down on what was left there, the twisted bedsheets and the portrait of the woman Dave had known in Lincoln. As I came through the door, Berne turned and made a blue fist at me. I say a blue fist because that's what it looked like. It was actually his normal-colored fist, but it was wrapped inside a blue scarf. "What is this?" he said.

"It looks like my scarf," I said.

"I thought you lost that scarf," he said.

"Yes," I said. "I thought so, too. Where did you find it?"

The fist tightened and took some of the creases out of the scarf. "I found it," he said, "in here. With Dave's things."

"Why would he have my scarf?"

"That's what I'm asking myself, Susan. Why would he have your scarf? And why would it be in the space between his bed and the wall?"

"I don't know," I said.

"You don't know," he said. "Do you know why he would write you a note saying that you would always be special to each other?"

"No," I said.

"And do you know why some of the guys downtown made jokes when he moved in here?"

"No," I said.

"Well, then you certainly don't know why those guys would say that once upon a time Dave and you were sneaking around?"

"No," I said. "What guys?"

"Ed," he said.

"Ed?" I said.

"Yes," he said. "He used to talk about you and Dave to anyone who would listen. He sounded proud. I think he imagined that you and Dave might end up together."

"When we were kids, maybe he liked me. Maybe he made up a story and told his father. But there's never been anything between me and Dave," I said.

"Am I a fool?" he said.

"No," I said.

It must have been the wrong thing to say because he stepped forward and hit me. Berne had never hit me before, so I didn't really understand what was happening. When I figured it out, I also thought that the scarf would cushion the blow. But his knuckle was poking out through a wrap, and it caught me right on the cheekbone, and I fell backward.

Berne stood over me. He was trembling. Then he unwrapped the scarf and threw it into the air. It opened up and came down slowly, like a parachute, and before it hit the ground he was gone from the barn.

I STAYED IN THE BARN for hours, sleeping on Dave's board bed until Sarah came over. I was crying, surprised that I was crying, but I stopped when she showed up. She took one look at my black eye and walked right out. I started crying again. "Stop that," she said, ducking her head back inside. "I'm just going to get something."

She came back with a makeup case and started putting foundation on my eye. "What a bastard," she said. "What a fool."

"He's not a fool," I said.

"If you don't think so, maybe you're one, too," she said.

The makeup was cool on my skin.

"Why do they call it black and blue?" I asked.

"Is this a riddle?" she said.

"No. I just want to know. It has red in there and brown, and when it heals, it will go to green and yellow."

"Tell me again what happened?" she said.

I told her. When I got to the part about the note from Dave, she asked me what it said. I said I didn't remember exactly. "I mean, did it say where he was going?" she said. I shook my head no. She kept on with the makeup.

When I got to the part about the scarf, she stopped and closed up the makeup case.

"What?" I said. "Do I look okay now? Because I'm not going to give him the satisfaction of going back in there looking like I got hit."

"I have to tell you something," she said.

"What?" I said.

"I have to tell Berne something, too," she said.

"What?" I said.

"It was my scarf," she said.

"What was your scarf?"

"The scarf he found was mine."

"It was mine," I said. "I lost it. Did you take it from me?"

"No, Susan. You showed yours to me, and I liked it so much that I went and got the same one."

"So how did it end up in here?" I said.

She didn't say anything.

"Tell me," I said.

"I was here," she said.

"When? Since when are you and Dave speaking?"

"We're not just speaking," she said.

"I see," I said.

She could tell from my tone that I didn't believe her. "What?" she said. "You think I'm trying to cover up for you? I'm telling you. Dave and I are having a little thing."

"A little thing?" I said. "Isn't he your son?"

She must have heard something funny in my voice because she took me by the chin and looked me straight in the eye.

"My god," she said. "You're jealous."

Then she marched on up to the house to set the record straight.

WHEN I CAME IN, Berne was standing by the kitchen table. Sarah was standing by the door. Both of them had crazy looks in their eyes. I didn't know who had said what or who had done what, but I did know that there was a kitchen knife out on the counter about midway between them. The air was tight, like any moment one of them might go for the knife. I didn't think they would. But you never know when family is involved. They stood facing each other like that for a long time. "So," Berne said finally. "You expect me to believe that?"

"I expect you to believe what's true," said my sister.

"I believe what I know," Berne said. "And I have had enough of hearing what's true and what's not true from this family, from you and from your sister and from your husband."

I didn't dare say anything. I just kept edging toward the knife until I was the closest of the three of us. If there was sudden movement, I could lunge for it and throw it into the trash can, or run away with it, or threaten to do myself in unless they stopped fighting. I was concentrating so hard on the knife that I didn't see Berne take a step toward me. I flinched, expecting another blow.

Instead, he let out a soft cry. "I'm sorry," he said. "If you tell me to believe you, I should believe you. That's where my father went wrong."

"Your mother was lying, Berne."

"That was only half of the problem," he said. "The other half was that he didn't believe her. There are two sides to every story, and you always have to listen to the other one."

I took a deep breath against his chest and held him tight. He felt like a good man to me, a man who had acted in error and was trying to set things right.

"Laurel?" I said.

"Laurel," he said, and squeezed me close to him.

MY SISTER LEFT TOWN. She called me and told me she was leaving, and I knew from her tone that it wasn't just melodrama. "I'm going to Lincoln," she said.

"Are you looking for Dave?" I said.

"No," she said. "At least I don't think so. I just need to go somewhere for a while that isn't here."

Laurel was born six months later. Right up until the end, I thought she would be a boy. Berne never wavered on his prediction of a girl. When Laurel was only four months old, I got pregnant again. Now, I told Berne, I'll be able to use the boy's name.

"How do you know it's not another girl?" he said.

"You think it's another girl?" I said.

"No," he said. "I think you're right. I think it's a boy."

I dreamed about the boy who would be Laurel's little brother. I even had a name picked out. But then I got a card in the mail from my sister. I hadn't talked to her in months. The card had a photo that slipped out when I opened it; in the picture, she was standing by a window, holding a little baby that looked just about the same age as Laurel. She and the baby were as beautiful as a painting. *Can you imagine?* Sarah wrote. *Ed would be so proud. Not that he'll ever know. Or Dave, for that matter. I haven't seen him since I got to Lincoln. I heard he went to Boston or Philadelphia. So it's just me and my family.*

You know what's funny? she wrote. *I'm the mother and the grandmother. How many women can say that?*

I miss you, she wrote, *and I love you.*

I called the phone number on the card.

"Hi," I said.

"Hi," Sarah said.

"What's his name?" I said. I already knew the answer.

"Ed," she said.

"Yeah," I said. "I figured. That was the name I wanted."

"You wanted for what?"

"For my baby," I said.

"For Laurel?" she said. "What kind of sense does that make?"

"No, the second baby," I said.

"You're pregnant again?" she said. "Congratulations."

"But I wanted the name Ed," I said.

"Well," she said. "Maybe this one will be a girl also."

"Berne thinks it's a boy," I said.

"How are things?" she said.

"With Berne?" I said. "Oh, you know."

"That bad?" she said.

"No, no," I said. "They're good. He is who he is. He works so hard to get things right. Do you know that he hung the painting?"

"What painting?" she said.

"That portrait Dave left for me," I said. "One day I came home, and it was hanging in the kitchen. Berne went and got it framed and everything. I didn't say a word about it, and then a few days later we were eating dinner, and he looked up at it and said that he liked it. 'There's something about it,' he said."

"There is something about it," Sarah said. "Listen, I should go. I'm glad you called. And I'm sorry I took the name you wanted."

"That's okay," I said. "James isn't such a bad name for a little boy."

"No," she said. "It's not at all."

After I hung up, I went outside. It was cold, so I bundled up, and it wasn't until I got out there that I realized that I was wearing the blue scarf Berne had found in the barn. I hadn't been in the barn much since Dave left. Laurel was scared of it; I was, too, a little bit. But the cold stung, and suddenly the barn didn't seem like such a bad idea. I went in through the main door, brushing a web out of my face.

Dave's bed had been in the back of the barn. I stood where his bed had been and fingered the scarf. Then I thought about taking it off, throwing it high in the air, and counting until it came down. I wondered how high I could count before it reached the ground. But I didn't throw it. Instead, I imagined throwing it into the air, and counted in my head. I got to eight, then imagined throwing the scarf again. The second time I got to ten.

AGAINST SAMANTHA

THE YEAR KICKED OFF WITH AN EVENT THAT I FEEL CONFI-
dent describing as godly. There were floods in London that grew
the river to monstrous proportions; the banks were rendered
meaningless. I had an acquaintance there, and I heard about the
floods in a letter. "More than a dozen souls have perished in
the Thames," Edith wrote. "Strange as it may seem, all but one
were malign. Nature did its part to sweep the city clean. It was
a clarifying moment." A few days later, the moat at the Tower of
London, which had been drained midway through the last century, was completely refilled by the brute force of a flood wave.
On this topic, Edith was droller. "I suppose it wished to visit the
Tower," she wrote.

That was how the year began, and it continued on in that
headlong spirit. In February massive hailstones rained down in
both the south of England and the south of Nebraska, killing
eight all told. In April, Chicago was host to what became known
as the Pineapple Primary, in which more than sixty bombs were
lobbed into polling places and the Nineteenth Ward commit-

teeman was shot to death in front of his wife and daughter. The
murderess Ruth Snyder was executed at Sing Sing. Edith com-
mented upon these events in letters she sent me over the course
of the spring and summer. She had a healthy appetite for both
the global and the local, and a penchant for anything involving
death, destruction, or disruption. As she wrote in one of her mis-
sives, "Estonia changed from the mark to the kroon; Chang Tso-
lin was murdered in June. History is quite lyrical these days."
I celebrated my twenty-fifth birthday in early July, and when I
looked at that portion of life that stretched before me and that
which trailed behind me, I realized that I was in no condition
to do what I had promised to do, which was to marry Samantha
Noble, the beautiful girl who wanted to marry me, and who was,
as luck would have it, Edith's daughter.

I was in good with the family, as should be clear. And why
not? I had been good to their daughter. In return, she had been
good to me, in some ways more than others. Over the course of
the year, Samantha and I had courted, had promised ourselves to
one another, and, formalities dispensed with, had proceeded to
investigate one another carnally in a rather rapacious manner. We
held the line against the most fearsome of intruders, of course, until we did not: the surrender (or conquest, depending upon your
perspective) came shortly after my birthday, just as the Olympics
were beginning in Amsterdam. (They followed the winter games
in St. Moritz; I learned about both sets of Olympiads from Edith,
who had a thing for them.) My parents had settled me into a small
apartment in New York City that Samantha had never seen—how
could she have?—and one fine afternoon, after a walk through
Central Park, she sat on a bench and clutched her stomach with
a loud cry. When I asked if she needed a doctor, she shook her
head. "I just need to lie down for a few moments," she said. "Isn't

your apartment nearby?" The pain on her face had to be seen to be believed—or rather, I should never have seen it, and then I could have disbelieved it.

I led her upstairs. Her hand was hot inside mine. I put her on the daybed and sat down to read a bit of Calkins. I was deep into a chapter when I noticed that there were hands at the sides of my head, and that they were connected to arms, and that those arms were bare of any petticoat and connected to a body that was every bit as bare. "My stomach is feeling better," said Samantha, and took my hand as if to show me, though she missed her stomach by a good half-foot: a very good half-foot, as it turned out. Amelia Earhart had successfully taken an aircraft across the Atlantic just weeks before, and that was what Samantha recalled to me as she piloted me toward the daybed. I was powerless to think of anything but what she was showing me, and yet I thought mainly of her mother, Edith, who was at that moment sitting in her drawing room in London, innocently considering the recent declaration of Malta as a British dominion, entirely unaware of the fact that I was accessioning her daughter. I felt for that woman and what she did not know. And yet, what matter? A tidal wave had filled the Tower moat, and now one filled me. I dreamed of an airship crashing into an icy plain. I knew that something like that had happened near the North Pole, but within my dream the event seemed fully original.

The dream must have been pushed up right against my wakening, for I came into the morning light with a sharp fear. For starters, one of my thumbs was sore, as if it had been bent backward nearly to the breaking point, and that concerned me greatly until I remembered that it had. But, in addition, there was a pain in my right eye, and I had a cottonmouth, and my ears could not decode the sounds they heard. Samantha was sleeping beside me, and I began to put my symptoms in order so that I could convey them to her when she woke. I thought that perhaps I was catching whatever she had contracted that had caused her stomachache, and it was a few moments before I remembered that the stomachache had been contrived, and that the contrivance had in fact led directly to the events that had dried my mouth and bent my thumb. The eye and ear I could not account for entirely.

Samantha was not my first; there had been a lady of the evening I patronized during a trip to Lisbon some years earlier. But Samantha was the first among the girls who were considered proper matches—the right age, the right class, the right faith— and as she lay there on the daybed, I suddenly had a pang of hatred for her. A pang of hatred for myself followed close behind. The woman had made herself available to me in a manner that risked her reputation. What right did I have to judge her? And yet my contempt was indisputable: "the woman," as a way of referring to my beloved, my betrothed? Beastly. Perhaps the devil in me was broadening. I went to the window. The park was across the street and I tried to take it all in with one long stare. Was that even possible? I had read an article about that exact question; the author, a respected alienist and psychologist, had suggested that a duration of twenty seconds contributed most to the masonry of recollection, and that any longer study began to take bricks away. I looked for twenty-five seconds, looked away, remembered nothing, wondered if I had proven anything.

The lady in Lisbon had been the first. Someone else had been the second, and another someone else the third. Then came the fourth, a girl here in town, the older sister of a school friend, and that was when my brazenness began to turn back in on itself. That woman, the older sister, had a worldly air; she had spent a year in Lyon, which she called a magical city, though I came to realize that by magical she meant sensual, and by city she meant the garret of her older lover, a married painter who had her strip down and stand in the center of a large bare floor. His paintings were portraits of her that he later surrounded with antique grandeur—palaces, fountains, arches. I had seen one. It was terrible: quite realistic. It was through this woman that I met Samantha.

They had come together to a dinner party at my aunt's townhouse the previous winter. The woman and I were pretending that we only hardly knew each other, and asking the sorts of questions you would ask a person of new acquaintance: *Tell me again, have you been to France?* That excited her. As part of that ruse, she drew in Samantha, who had been a younger classmate of hers some years before. Samantha later said that she took one look at me and knew I was the man she would marry. I took one look at her and thought little, though when she turned to speak to someone else I do remember remarking to myself that she had the figure of an angel, particularly from the rear. I was by no means immune to that fact, or in general to the effect of a beautiful young woman with long blonde hair. She was demure and quiet for the entirety of that first dinner engagement, and as we parted, she took my hand and said that she was pleased to meet me, and I went home with the other woman and we ruined one another additionally. A few days later, the other woman was scheduled for another visit, and she did appear, but with a restless look in her eyes that was nevertheless devoid of hunger. I asked her what seemed to be the matter, and she told me she was laying down her arms because Samantha was in love with me. It was such a preposterous excuse that I knew it to be true. Four months later, Samantha and I were betrothed to one another.

Samantha came on quickly at first. She was beautiful, and that made me the envy of many men of many ages, and I enjoyed the warmth of their covetousness. She was ardent, which kept me distracted, and she was faithful, which meant that I did not have to account for a time when that ardent spirit would alight elsewhere. I took her attentions as she wished me to, which is to say that I took them for granted. I met her family during those first months—though by family I should say her parents, because she had no siblings. They were visiting in the States before heading back to London. Her father, Herman, was a stern, handsome, fatally superior man who had started as a butcher and grew a small empire in the north of England. He liked to speak of the "black branches of being that hung down low in the minds of men." He wanted a poetical effect around him, and I suppose that he got it. Her mother was Edith, whom I mentioned before. At first, Edith was nervous, or seemed to be: her eyes darted from spot to spot in the room, though it was her own hotel room, and not much of it could have come as a surprise to her.

After we took coffee and biscuits in the room, we got to talking, the four of us. Her father had much to say about Trotsky's exile to Turkestan, a punishment he believed was severally insufficient, both as penalty for past infractions and as deterrence to similar-minded radicals. He had many friends who had gone over the edge politically. "It is a curse of our race," he said, his face so grim that I nearly laughed. Samantha tended to agree with her father in matters such as these, but her beauty both camouflaged her hard edge and rendered it all the more surprising when it appeared. Edith, unlike her husband and daughter, displayed both a lightness of touch and a heavy ethical hand, and she negotiated one against the other deftly. She liked to make witty remarks that seemed like mere decoration but gained substance under scrutiny. An example: The Chinese founded an Academy of Art in March.

"Oh," she said, "and to think they have their own art, too." It sounds like the statement of a flibbertigibbet, but that is because I cannot possibly convey the finely wrought combination of irony, condescension, and even hostility toward the idea that such news should surprise anyone. "The West rests on its own sense of its uniqueness, but that uniqueness is only another word for novelty, and novelty is only another word for repeating the past without acknowledging that repetition." She did not say that, but she might as well have: It was all woven into the tapestry of her remark. There were other examples I cannot recall at the moment; I remember only the kindness of her face as she made them, and the activity at the corners of her eyes and mouth that made that kindness count. She was the smartest woman I had ever met, and she was the mother of the woman I was to marry.

When Herman rediscovered his biblical distaste for America and the two of them sailed back to England, I stood with Samantha dockside and waved. I was smiling, but it was only at Herman's departure. I experienced Edith's loss almost surgically and drew closer to Samantha to allay the pain I felt. Edith must have sensed it, too, because her letters began to arrive at once. It pleased Samantha that her mother had such a favorable impression of me, though the two of them had an ambivalent relationship. Samantha wanted her mother's wisdom but feared the rest: she worried that the ravages of time would erase her beauty, which was substantial, and turn her into something more ordinary. "We all become our mothers," she said, by way of apology. I did not tell her that I was banking on it.

I have not spoken of my livelihood, have I? This seems like an appropriate juncture. I am a junior manager in a bank. My uncle is the president of the bank, so there is every expectation that I will rise through the ranks and become an officer of the institution. That will make me a wealthy man by forty, and a comfort-able man long before that. When she visited the bank, Samantha told me that she did not care about money, but by now she has said it so frequently that there is no way to believe her. Edith, on the other hand, cared about worldly things only insofar as they informed her understanding of the world, and she proved it all the time. I once saw her put a dollar bill in a tree. "I want to see if it is here tomorrow," she said with a straight face. "Maybe a bird will use it to buy some eggs." Again, a joke that revealed a deeper truth.

That morning when I woke and stood by the window, I re-turned and sat at the breakfast table in my apartment and consid-ered what had transpired the night before. Samantha had taken me, or at the very least she had taken me to a place where I had taken her. And now, hours later, I was in a small space with a woman I had possessed, and I still smelled her on my hands and face, and I still remembered the way she had opened her mouth to meet my open mouth, and yet I did not feel an ounce of kind-ness toward her. I had a schoolmate who used to say that he had "throbbed off into" a woman, a phrase I found reprehensible at the time, but which I found useful the morning after I had throbbed off into Samantha. I retreated from the window and found one of Edith's letters. I sat on the bed and reread it. Her hand was steady and her mind more so. I treasured her opinion on everything from Hirohito to Mickey Mouse. When Charles Lindbergh had received the Medal of Honor for his first trans-atlantic flight, she had confessed to me that she found the man "frightfully repulsive, not just for his ideas but for his single-mindedness of purpose—I would have preferred that he fly off in all directions at once." Her daughter, for all her beauty, for all her youth, accounted Lindbergh a hero. That saddened me. Despite that, I was pledged, and her scent was on my hands and face, and one day soon I would marry her.

How can a day like that be forestalled? I considered jumping out of the window, though I was only on the third floor and would most likely embarrass rather than extinguish myself. I considered paying one of my schoolmates to seduce Samantha, after which time I could denounce her as unfaithful and promiscuous, though that seemed rather too Byzantine a scheme, not to mention that I did not wish to crush her spirit, only to free my own. I had no real sense of my options and no real belief in my freedom. This may not make for much of a story, and yet it is every story, told all the time, in every language, with every available flourish. Man is asphyxiated by choice, not in the abstract but in the concrete. It hardens around him.

I went back to sleep, where I had a dream. I was riding on a bicycle. A beautiful young woman with long blonde hair was sitting on my lap. I was facing forward. She was facing me. She had on a white skirt, and I reached up underneath it and felt the presence of nothing additional. "Lift it," she said, and I did, and she joined us together with a gasp. This was my betrothed, I was sure, and the prospect of being joined to her in this way each and every night for the rest of my life suddenly seemed less odious. There was transport involved. I kept riding, fast at first and then slower and slower until my feet were going around in a nearly frozen circle. The bike remained upright. She put her arms around my neck and spoke my name. Then she spoke her own. It was Edith. This time, I did not wake with a start. I slid down into the bed of sleep and, having arrived there, tried to climb back up the incline to my dream. I saw my salvation, finally. My dream would protect me. My dream would keep time from moving forward ruthlessly, from suffocating my sense of my self, from forcing me to come into the world as someone else. I regained sleep, and then the corner of my dream. We biked on, over a long cobblestone path, the unevenness of which was wonderful for both of us. She asked me to tell her what was up ahead. "Black branches," I said, and she laughed. There were no black branches and she knew it. What there was, which she didn't know, was a place where the road ended, or at least dropped off into a shallow stream. I rode on into the water. We slowed down again and nearly stopped. The bike was upright in the shallows. The water began to rise. Edith's arms tightened around me. Heat came out of her mouth and her chest and from between her legs. The water was cold. I knew it, but even when it had reached the bottom of my feet I experienced it only as an idea. The dream gave no indication of ending; inside it I thanked Edith, and she threw back her head and delivered a laugh I can describe only as godly. I matched her laugh, there in the dream. Did I laugh outside it? Did I disturb the sleeping Samantha? I did not know and I was not about to surface and find out.

THE HUNTER AND
THE HUNTED

Dear X,

I am not writing to you. I am writing to your letter. It is sitting on the table in front of me, white paper, black type that looks like it came from an old typewriter, your signature streaking across the bottom of the page. Why am I writing to your letter and not to you? For focus and also for protection: protection for us both. Dear letter, I attack. Dear letter, I relent. My wife is out of the house. I have time for this now. I should get on with it.

Writing a letter to another letter may sound questionable, but it is a deep conviction of mine. It is related to a trick I learned when I was a waiter. I would tell customers, "Do not direct your anger toward me. Speak to me, but let your anger flow toward the menu." It started as a joke—I had a series of belligerent patrons who drove me to the edge of retaliation—but it grew into a kind of belief system. The restaurant's soul did reside in the menu. It was a record of what was and what could not be. I was only a messenger. Do not kill the messenger. Do not even address him. Direct your attention toward the text. Make peace, or war, with what is written.

I relayed this philosophy to hundreds of customers during my last years at the restaurant. Some found it charming, because they understood my aim. Some found it presumptuous, because they subscribed to another philosophy—that servants should not think above their station. One of the members of this latter camp complained to my boss, and I was fired. My dismissal launched me into my new life, into real estate, into wealth. I became a husband to a woman who was an equal match for me in ambition and intelligence. She did not want to have children, and I agreed, imagining that we might be happy together. I could not have imagined any of this while I was working in the restaurant. In retrospect, I am thankful I was fired, for all these reasons. At the time, I was stung. I wanted a fair hearing but I received none. Only a single sous chef shed a tear for me. Her name was Clementine. Much later, after I came to America, I learned that song: Oh my darling, oh my darling, oh my darling Clementine. A little while after that, I met you. I told you that if we ever had a child together, we'd name her that. I assumed it would be a daughter, a little girl who looked like you. I was talking in the heat of new love. We were sitting by the water. There was a gap of bench between us. You never liked to sit too close to me. Once I asked why and you said, "The space between us represents your wife." You spoke slowly and deliberately, as if lecturing a child on safety measures—which, in a sense, you were.

My wife would have known exactly what to call this space between people that represents another person. Her vocabulary is and has always been the most impressive thing about her. "It's true that I love words," she said. "But all this time I've believed that my interest in finding the exact right word for a situation was just an adventitious bonus." In a less serious woman, this would have been a joke, but she intended, as she would say, not a soupçon of levity.

Dear X,

Direct your attention toward the primary document. In my case, the primary document is the letter you have written me. It was written ten days ago, mailed nine days ago, received six days ago, left to cool off on my counter for one day, and then read with hands that somehow manufactured a steadiness that I did not, deep down, possess. Its message was clear: you did not want to see me again, would not be my lover, could not be my friend. "I am gone," you wrote, "like the dodo." I called you when I received this letter because I wanted to tell you that I loved you. I did not tell you anything of the sort. Instead, I agreed with you that you needed to be gone. "Like the dodo," I said

"After this call, no more me," you said.

"Understood," I said. I was gripping the phone so hard that I hoped it might break.

"You know why," you said. "Right?"

"No," I said. I was stalling.

"The pain," you said. "But the pleasure is part of it, too. I need it all off the table."

"So let's clear the table," I said.

"Well, no," you said. "That makes it sound like a clean slate, and like something might be later put there. The whole table has to be gone, and everything around it, too. There can't be things that are next to the table, waiting to be lifted up and placed there. There can't be anything. There has to be nothing. I am saying this as much to myself as to you."

"I was just following your metaphor," I said.

"I know," you said. "I'm not sure I'm finding the right words. I've gone through it all. I went through accepting the side deal. I went through hating you. I went through her-or-me, and play-me-or-trade-me. I don't know where I am now, or what to call it. I just know that it has to be far from you, and that there has to be a high wall between us. I have to go."

"I have to go," I said.

"What?" you said. "You mean hang up?"

"Yes," I said. "That sounds right."

"Jesus," you said. Your voice sharpened. "Is your wife home? I thought I heard a door close."

"Okay," I said. "That sounds great." I paused. "Yes. It's the corner building. I just have a few pieces of furniture up on the roof-deck: two chairs and a table. There's an umbrella, but I think I can remove it before you get there. Nine o'clock, you said?"

"You're an asshole," she said.

"That's right," I said. "Off the table." I hung up the phone. My hand was cramped from clutching it so hard. I opened it and closed it experimentally. My wife was not home. She was working late. That's what happens when you are a lawyer for a publishing firm and the other lawyer in your department has a child and decides to work from home and then, as the months go on, to hand over enough responsibilities that it becomes clear that the rest of the responsibilities will soon follow. You—if you are the remaining lawyer, if you are my wife—step into the breach. You stay late. You go to the office on Saturdays. You explain to your husband that the two of you are happiest when you are working—you at your office, he at his property-management firm—and you remind him that when the two of you had too much time on your hands, a kind of restlessness infected the marriage. "Our conversations then were an invidious reminder of how poorly we were addressing our own needs," my wife once said. She leaves me notes in the morning when she leaves, and I put notes on top of her notes when I go to sleep. We communicate through these documents: the primary, the secondary, the others. This is why I am happy writing a letter to your letter. I have years of training in these matters.

Dear X,

Why did I let you believe that my wife was home when she was not? Because it would injure you. Why did I want to injure you? Because you had injured me. You wanted to take it off the table, all of it, despite the fact that for nearly two years it had sustained me. When I met you, my wife and I were going through a difficult period. I told her that it was the hell of adjusted expectations. She frowned and said that we were "above timberline." It was not the right time for her fluency. I took a deep breath, sat down on the bed, and said that I was not sure that I loved her, that despite all that she had meant to me, I just could not see around the corner.

A few days later, I met you. It was at an open house for one of my properties. Usually I don't attend them myself, but it was a weekend filled with bad weather, and I needed somewhere to go. I let Janice, the agent, off the hook, and told her I would cover it myself. "Thank you, Mr. Ramirez," she said. She yawned and stretched. Janice has always had a thing for me, and she's beautiful, but I was never the type to run around. When I started off in business, they used to call me "Play-It-Safe Paco," though in fact usually I did not play it at all. I held my residential properties for years, let their value grow slowly, like a tree rather than a flower — there was not always as much beauty in the process as there could have been, but there was a thick trunk and there were roots. I behaved similarly in my dealings with women. When Janice yawned and stretched, when she pressed her body against the fabric of her clothes, I cannot face.

Janice left. I stayed. The apartment was a small two-bedroom with a bath and a half. The master bedroom was big and had one large walk-in closet. The kitchen had just been redone with a beautiful marble counter. The fireplace didn't work, but the detailing on it was exquisite. I showed the place to a gay couple, then a straight couple, then to a man who was in the middle of a divorce. He was the most interested, and also the most interesting—he touched everything and shook his head, as if he were trying to rouse himself from a fog. He thought he'd put in an offer. "I just wish I knew what direction things were going to take," he said. "I am ninety percent sure that I'm going to need to buy my own place, but that ten percent really weighs on me." I wished him luck. I was sitting on a folding chair I had brought, reading a *Blood-Horse* magazine— since I was a little boy, I have always wanted to own thoroughbreds, though now that I have the money to do so I realize that I don't know nearly enough about it, and I am always trying to bring myself to the point where I feel, if not confident, at least competent enough to make a purchase. I collect art instead, because I know a little about it, because it gives me pleasure.

A knock came at the door.

A small woman was standing in the hallway. It was you. As you came into the room, I revised my first impression. You were short, certainly, but you were not skinny, and you had a presence, partly as a result of your beautiful arms and partly because of your enormous eyes. Neither was adventitious. "Karen Lewis," you said, and extended your hand.

"Francisco Ramirez," I said.

"That's a very grand name," you said.

"Well, I am a nobleman," I said.

"Really?"

"No," I said. "Only a rich man."

You laughed. Perhaps you thought I was joking, I realized later. You had no way of knowing that I owned not only this apartment but nearly two thousand others. You had no way of knowing that I was worth ten thousand times as much as when I first came to the United States, fresh from a short but not entirely unsuccessful career as a waiter and restaurant manager, or that earlier in that career I was so poor that I sometimes had to steal from customers. I would like to say that the stealing was infrequent. The truth was that it was nearly constant. When I told my wife about it, she stared off into the middle distance and then returned with a vocabulary lesson. "Stealing and robbery are different," she said. "Stealing is related to words like 'stealthy.' When you steal, you're trying to escape detection. Robbery's very different. That's when you confront someone and take something by force." I'm sure she was right, or mostly right. At the very least, I could not argue with her. English was not my first language. If I had told you about my early transgressions, I do not think that you would have come back at me with surgery performed on my words. You would have judged me, or loved me, or both. I did not tell you about my stealing. You did not lift your lovely arms over your head. We stood professionally near one another, and I manufactured enough concentration to speak about the central air and the marble countertop.

You did not like the apartment. You felt that the closet was situated awkwardly in the master bedroom, and that the whole place was overpriced. I made a mental note to call the gay couple and tell them the apartment was theirs if they wanted it. On the way out, you picked up the *Blood-Horse* magazine, inspected the cover, put it back down. You paused by the door to tell me about yourself. You were a painter, beginning to acquire a reputation.

Your father was a rich man, "like you," you said, maybe believing it a little bit more this time. You had been engaged to one of your painting teachers, but it hadn't worked out.

"Why?" I said. "If you don't mind my asking."

"You can ask anyone anything anytime," you said.

One week later, we were lovers.

Dear X,

I fold your letter, unfold it, read it again, refold it. I have done this four or five times over the past hour. They say that you should keep your friends close and your enemies closer. The letter did not bother me so deeply when I first received it. As I have said, I called to talk things through. No part of it was unexpected. We had been weakening each other for months, especially since we stopped sleeping together. I realize that I have skipped from the moment when we became lovers to the moment when we stopped sleeping together. Between that is a gap. I will protect this period, not from shame, not from fear, but from love and from a fierce sense of obligation.

I can sketch what happened, but the sketch will not satisfy even the most casual reader. We were together. My marriage was stalled. I was making more money than ever, and enough that I could suddenly see clear to pay for any arrangement that might transpire: wife and mistress, ex-wife and girlfriend, ex-wife and new wife. One day, in bed, I made you an offer to come across to me. You refused. We lost and then regained our breaths. I asked again later, when you were not sitting astride me, when your face was not stretched with pleasure. You refused again. I backed off, nursed my wounds, waited a day, made another attempt, was rebuffed again, feared that the reopened wounds would never heal.

I should have stopped making offers, but I could not, in this case, play it safe. You could say that it was a fatal flaw, but in fact it was the opposite: that was the one part of my life where I stayed the flaw and surged forward hopefully. Whenever I saw you, even if it was just for a casual drink or a cup of coffee, I felt an almost over-whelming sense of desire. You reported similar trouble, and we blamed each other, and we fought. And so I knew the day would come when either you would break or I would, and the broken party would ask the other party to release him or her forever. You broke. I fully believed that in time we would be lovers again. I felt the unfairness of the circumstance pulling at me. Once, when the pain was nearly too high to bear, I told my wife a version of the story, pretending that it had happened to an old acquaintance of mine back in Spain. "He suffered not just from his circumstance," I said, "but from the anxiety that his circumstance might not have been unique in any way. Is there a word for that?"

"Pipe organs have devices called tremulants that create vi-brato in the note," she said. "At some point, time serves as a trem-ulant: everything that happens is just the minor recurrence of something that has happened." It wasn't exactly what I was look-ing for, but she seemed so happy that I didn't object.

About a month ago, you and I met for drinks. We were not the only ones meeting. Since we stopped sleeping together, we have worked hard to construct a social structure around us that will permit us to remain in each other's company. We have one or two mutual friends in business (my business) or in the art world (your art world). I have continued to collect, a pursuit that stretches my wife to the bounds of her indifference, and so she permits me to go out by myself and sit with what she calls the "albinic syba-rites." At some point there is no dividend in following her lan-guage. Even if someone had called my wife and reported exactly

who was sitting around the table, it would not arouse suspicion.
A fifty-year-old collector with a sixty-year-old gallery owner, a
forty-year-old journalist, and a thirty-year-old painter? The composition was perfect.

At this particular drink, you were nervous. Or rather: we were
nervous, but you were showing it. We had been through a month
of not speaking, and then a month of speaking every day, and then
a day when you called me to say that you could not go through
another month like it. "But it's making me happy," I said.

You sighed. "It's making me miserable. I love talking to you.
But I don't talk to a man every day unless I'm sleeping with him."

"Okay," I said.

"Not okay," you said.

The next night was the drink. You should have been asking the
gallery owner about his fall shows. I should have been talking to
the journalist and trying to extract the names of next season's hot
prospects. Instead, we spoke mainly to each other. At one point, the
waitress asked us if we wanted more drinks, and I ordered for you.
I am sorry. It was instinct. It doesn't matter, anyway. No one noticed, not even the journalist, and after the second round of drinks,
the conversation broadened, and there was nothing left for the others to notice. Around eleven, the party broke up. I wanted to walk
with you a few blocks uptown before I got in a cab. You said no. It
was cold outside. You wanted to go home and go to sleep. I insisted,
and prevailed; we sat in a small restaurant and you drank coffee.
"You didn't even come to the show," I said. I had converted one of
my vacant apartments into a gallery, and I was showing work by
Spanish painters I had collected over the years. The journalist had
called it "a small show that produces large pleasures."

"I was busy," you said.

"You weren't busy," I said. "There was a woman there who

said she had been at a drink with you just a half hour before."

"I didn't feel like coming," you said. "I think that maybe you acquired some of those paintings because they reminded you of me."

"What?" I said. "That's idiotic." But it was not idiotic. There was one portrait in particular, painted by a seventy-year-old Castilian, that looked almost exactly like you. If you had mentioned it specifically, I would have lied and said that I had owned that painting for years. I was not proud that you had turned my head far enough that I was buying paintings that looked like you.

"Maybe," you said. She looked defeated. "All I know is that I didn't want to be there, and I don't really want to be here."

"The show was important to me," I said. "I would have liked it if you had made an appearance."

"I know," you said. "I'm sorry." You looked like you might cry.

"I thought we were going to try to do well by one another," I said. "If we're not, then there are many other things we should discuss."

"Like what?" you said.

"Like the new man," I said. You had been to Los Angeles for a show of your work, and while you were there, you had started sleeping with a young doctor. He came to visit at least once a month, and while you told me without provocation that you weren't in love with him, you also made it clear that you had no intention of ending things. It seemed that he was the perfect lover, at least for the moment. He did not live where you lived. He did not see you often enough, or for long enough, for you to grow bored, or to feel afraid that you were not feeling love—or worse, that you were. The perfection had a cost, which is that he was not in any true sense a real person. He was a coat you bought off the rack, an unsuperlative fashion statement. He was an appurtenance. When I told you that, your face darkened. You did not like me using my wife's words.

"That's it," you said, and got into a taxicab. The evening had begun light and ended with a thud. I went home. I slipped into bed. My wife was there, which was a rarity those days. Her work must have ended early. She slid back toward me. It was warm in the bed. That was where I belonged, and I told myself that until I believed it.

Dear X,

After I insulted you by insulting your new lover, after you stormed off to your taxicab, you disappeared. You wouldn't answer my phone calls. I grew afraid that we would never speak again, and my fear drove me into irrational behavior. I dialed six digits of your phone number and hung up. I wrote your name on a piece of paper, over and over again, as if that might summon you. I went to the apartment where we had met, which was vacant again—the gay couple had decided to move to the suburbs and adopt a baby—and I sat in the middle of the floor and I thought I might cry. Then I went home, and went to bed with my wife, and never stopped thinking about you. Time passed like that for a while. Then, one day, there was a birthday party for a mutual friend. The guest of honor was a woman who was known both for her superb taste in contemporary art and for the massive fortune she had inherited from her father, who had founded the nation's largest manufacturer of railway machinery. Her gallery was called, in tribute, Stacker. I asked my wife to go to the party, but she said she'd be at the office late. "I'll probably be home early," I said. "I get tired when I'm at parties without you. I feel weakened."

"Etiolated," she said. "There's a word for it."

I went to the party, thrilled to think I might see you. I started

talking to a woman who owned a small gallery. You came up behind me and dug a fingernail into my side. "Hi," you said.

"Ow," I said.

"Louis is here," you said.

"Louis?"

"The guy from California." I was being tested. I had failed
before, so I chose to pass. You introduced me as a friend and a collector. I shook Louis's hand. "Nice to meet you," I said.

"I don't know anything about art," he said. "All of it looks
good to me, or bad, depending on my mood. I can't tell if there's
any real good or bad in it."

You excused yourself to go to the ladies' room. "She's been
talking about you for the last few months," I said. "She seems
thrilled to see you." I did not see the harm in supporting him. I
doubted he would last, but I could not see the point of contribut-
ing to his demise. How would that work to my advantage?

When he got up to get more drinks, you finished your wine
with exaggerated quickness. "I was thinking maybe I would
break up with him this weekend," you said. "Or maybe not." It is
not an exaggeration to say that you were happier than I had ever
seen you. Nor is it an exaggeration to say that you were incomplete without your sadness.

"I thought we weren't talking about those things anymore,"
I said.

"You're right. Not allowed. If we follow the rules, there's some
chance we might not grow to hate each other."

The birthday girl floated by, and I went to speak with her. From
the corner of my eye, I watched you and Louis. He handed you
your wine. You put your head on his shoulder. His hand went to
your head. Your face, which I had looked upon hundreds of times
with something more than hope, disappeared inside the crook of

his arm. I think his hands were between your knees. I was about to come back and sit, but the two of you stood. You walked up to me, smiling. "We're going to head home," you said.

"Nice to meet you," Louis said.

The next person I spoke to was. . . . . . I cannot remember. Some young woman with a story about how her libido was the brightest color on the broader canvas of her life, I'm guessing. I was not feeling rage or sorrow or loss. I was feeling maturity. I had watched a man claim you, and I had thought mainly of your happiness and how you might truly secure it. My sense of things curdled into superiority and then drained away entirely. "Good-bye," I said to the young woman I was probably talking to.

On the walk home, it occurred to me that I might be married forever, to the same woman, that we might have an endless series of ups and downs, that they might be a condition of our existence, in the way the sea is the condition of a boat's existence. I thought about you at home, in your apartment, undressing for your visitor. Would he stand looking at your paintings rather than at you? That would be a wonderfully modest evasion, almost strategic.

My wife was not home when I arrived. I poured myself a drink and sat up waiting for her, paging through a *Blood-Horse* magazine. Something was wrong with the magazine. The pages were printed with a poorer quality of ink. The horses looked sickly. Something had tainted the finest bloodlines. I put the magazine away and took out the dictionary. I was looking for a word that described what I was feeling. I had no intention of using it. I just needed to know. And I needed to find it on my own. There was no asking my wife. There was no asking anyone anything anymore.

FROM THE FRONT

Dear Isabel,

You have no doubt seen, and perhaps even read, the new history of warfare that is all the rage with the fashionably intelligent among today's youth. I figure in that book. In the section on advances in muzzle-loaded ammunition, the book describes me as a codeveloper, with Delvigne, of the Minié ball. This strikes me as something of a joke. Do the authors of this wretched tome really think that Delvigne did anything other than drink too much wine and sleep late and run his hands up under nurses' skirts while whistling Méhul? The man was a riot of mustache and dirty shirts. I wish they would not malign me by comparing my contribution with his. I was pleased to be his brother-in-arms and to be his tentmate and to be his dinner companion and to be his sympathetic ear, but I will never be his equal. Rather: *he* will never be mine.

I am sorry, Isabel. I send you only a single letter each year, and I have already let my distemper get the best of me. Let me be more measured in my comments. Delvigne was not a brainless heap of skin, bones, and blood. He did contribute to the invention of the Minié ball, but the way in which he contributed has never been properly explained. The Minié ball is named after me for a reason. I will tell you and only you that reason, because of your mother and how much you resemble her. The fact that you never had occasion to meet that woman is perhaps the only imperfect thing about you.

We were in a tent, Isabel. It was spacious because all the tents for officers were spacious. Soldiers threw them up in groups of nine or twelve or fifteen, depending upon the size of the war party. The captains' tents were always in the front row, which looked out onto the battlefield, and I had a subordinate, one tent back, whose job was to operate the telegraph in case I shouted a message. The message might be to the effect that the enemy was sending an officer to negotiate and I wanted to know what I was entitled to promise. The message might be to the effect that I was sending a man out to meet the railcars that were bringing supplies. That day I was asking the telegraph operator to send a message to another encampment one hundred miles east and inquire about the weather. I needed to know.

"I'll bet it's raining there, too," Delvigne grumbled. He had his coat stretched over his head because the night before he had indulged excessively. The condition of his mustache attested to the extreme nature of his evening. Any man would have laughed at Delvigne. We were stationed in northern Africa, where we were campaigning with the French chasseurs, and rain was a rarity. We had rain that day, and so it was fair to expect that we would not have rain for much longer. But I did not laugh. Rather, I shouted to the operator and told him to cancel the message; the moment that Delvigne spoke I became certain that it was in fact raining. Delvigne never got the weather wrong. This was only one of his talents: he was also a powerful chess player, a crack shot, and the strongest officer I knew. He was prodigious in many ways, to be sure. But he was lazy and dissolute and preferred to lounge in bed carping about his headache and remembering the scent of the previous night's nurse. So I shouted to the operator and told him to cancel the telegraph. This drew a laugh from Delvigne, and that was followed by a long groan. Delvigne told me that he believed he was suffering from more than the pain of the previous night. "I think I am burning alive from fever," he said. "My eyes are boiling in my head. I remember when my dear departed mother would care for me." He retched off to the side of the bed, into an upside-down hat. "Boiling," he said.

Here I should pause, while you think about this single point of similarity between Delvigne and yourself: both lost mothers young. For many years, this was not a point of pitiful pride with Delvigne; he had not always been a sot and a fool. Fifteen years earlier, he was a capable commander who dressed sharply, had nearly perfect recall when it came to the recent military history of the nation, and was so fleet of foot that he could outrun a horse over a distance of one kilometer. I am not employing hyperbole here. In March of 1835, Captain Henri-Gustave Delvigne outran a horse for one kilometer and had enough time left over to scramble up a tree and leap down from a branch onto the bare back of the horse he had just bested. Now that was a soldier! That was a man! He had a taste for the ladies, but the ladies had a taste for him in return. I had heard tales of Delvigne's appetites; I remember remarking to another captain that if I had a daughter I would not object if she ended up arranged compromisingly on Delvigne's divan. I do not feel that way any longer, but I am not as far from it as I imagined I might be when my feelings started to change. If you, my dear one, responded to this letter with a brief note,

"Father: With Delvigne," I would feel only a twinge of rage rather than the consuming spasm that would be more appropriate to the news. Delvigne was, as I have said, a man with substance.

All of this, and a designer of tools of war as well. Back in those days, Delvigne contrived of a rifle barrel with a separate gunpowder chamber located at the breech and separated from the rest of the barrel by a rigid metal lip. After powder was packed into that chamber, a round bullet was pushed down the barrel and hammered into place with a ramrod, an act which, while flattening the bullet to fit the rifling grooves, also distorted it so that it flew crooked when fired. To permit continued use of this type of barrel, Delvigne invented a new shape for the bullet—it was longer and cylindrical, and expanded more evenly when beaten with the ramrod. This was an improvement, but not enough of an improvement, and the army did not take it up. Instead, they adopted a rifle designed by Colonel Louis-Etienne de Thouvenin, who had in fact only slightly modified Delvigne's design. It was as if a painter had added a mole to the face of a portrait and was credited with the entire canvas. Delvigne was not bitter. In those days he had no need to be. He was a man with everything around him. He went back to his perfectly tailored coats, to his wine, and to the women who awaited him when he returned home from the field of battle.

Now, we come to the irony: if Delvigne was slighted to a small degree in the popular account of the first phase of development, he was overly credited to a great degree in the second phase. I was the arms master in that northern African camp where I was stationed with Delvigne, and weekly I took several shipments of rifles and bullets, and it was not uncommon for the soldiers to complain about inaccurate flight. "I cannot listen to the carping," Delvigne said to me. "When a man does for his army one tenth of what I have done, then I will listen to him, but only then. Meanwhile, bring me a wineglass and a nurse: you fill the one and I will fill the other."

I took his words as a challenge. The thought of Delvigne listening! On one of those rare rainy days, I was trapped inside the tent alone. That was the moment inspiration chose to appear to me. It occurred to me that perhaps the best way to create a bullet that would keep its shape when hammered in—and not, afterward, lose its shape again when the powder blew out of the compartment near the breech and into the barrel—was to make it cylindrical, with a hollow base and a pointed tip. When the powder caught, the fire and expanding gases would enlarge the skirting of the bullet enough to align with the grooves of the inside of the barrel and seal the barrel beneath the bullet to ensure maximum accuracy. I went away from the tent through the rain to the company's smith, and I asked him to fashion a few of these bullets. He complied, and I brought those bullets back to the tent and placed them on top of an envelope that contained a note for Delvigne. "Captain," it began, "here is a type of bullet that I have invented. I have simultaneously built upon the foundation you laid and razed the structure erected by Thouvenin, who is a scoundrel and a traitor and, from what I hear, a silent player in the symphony of love, if you take my meaning: he endeavors with all his might to bring sound out of his instrument but cannot." The note was folded in neat thirds like a proper letter. I was and have continued to be meticulous in that regard.

That was when Delvigne returned to the tent. He did not read my letter. (I hope that you do not make that same mistake, my dear. If this letter is down in a pile, neglected, it will cause me unimaginable pain.) He lay down in the tent, clutched his head, and told me that he was sicker than he had ever been. When I asked the telegraph operator to check the weather, Delvigne called out that he expected more rain and then lapsed back into illness. He retched off the side of the bed, filling his hat. I waited for him to ask me about my morning, at which time I would have told him that I thought I had solved the problem of the rifle bullets. But he did not ask. He moaned and clutched his head some more. As I have said, he was not the brave soldier I had heard about through my youth. He writhed as if in the grips of a fit. He called out piti-fully the names of women he had loved. He prayed for them to come and save him. The one he called for most passionately was named Isabel. I never knew the woman, never even received a description of her, but the way in which Delvigne wailed for her stuck to my heart like a stubborn burr, and when I saw you that first day of your life, and my soul went out to you with the pur-est love I have ever known, I knew that your name should be Isabel.

Delvigne eventually stopped calling for Isabel and then for all the women. In the afternoon, a doctor stopped by: a corporal in an adjoining tent had heard Delvigne's cries and thought to summon medical help. The doctor touched Delvigne's forehead, felt around his neck, and then declared that there was very little he could do. Delvigne, he explained, had contracted an infection that had colonized most of his body. The second he left, Delvigne began to thrash more violently. Blood welled up in his nose. His eyes snapped open. He recognized me. "Captain Minié," he said. "Please help me." His entire body began to shiver. His eyes were a fearsome shade of yellow. "Captain," he said, "reach beneath my bed and find a rifle." I did not move, so he bent down and produced the rifle himself. "The powder is already loaded. Will you shoot me?" he said. I ignored the request and looked away. He followed my gaze, which had quite accidentally landed on the bullets that I had designed. He reached out a sweaty arm and gathered the bullets into his palm. He looked at them. "Hollow base," he said. "Nice." He slid one into the barrel, weakly took a ramrod into his hand, and pounded the bullet down. He was turning the rifle around when his finger slipped and pulled the trigger. The shot was deafening on the tent. The bullet came out of the barrel with a severe leftward deviation. Delvigne began to make a noise that was halfway between a laugh and a sob. "There should be an iron plug into the base." Then he lapsed into a silence that seemed to my untrained eye like a coma.

When the doctor returned, I did not mention the shot. It seemed undignified, at least. The doctor loaded Delvigne onto a narrow cot and carried him out of the tent. After a while I reached for a piece of paper. Delvigne's ravings had given me an idea. With the smith's help, I improved upon my own invention by the addition of a small iron plug in the bullet's hollow base that, on firing, would be propelled upward to help shape the bullet and strengthen the tip as the skirting flattened out. I left northern Africa early the next week, while Delvigne was still recuperating, and though I thought for a time that he might die, I had not correctly estimated his physical capabilities. He fought his infection for weeks but recovered nearly to perfect health, was discharged from military service, and married a young woman who was an actress on the Paris stage. This was just before Delvigne took her to America and tried to make his fortune in the West, which means that it was just before he went mad. They say that the fever that almost took him in the tent may have lain in wait inside his mind for years, springing forth at a later date without any warning. His life became a series of irrational connections and concoctions. He came to believe that the Americans were fighting for French independence. He believed that his wife was also a character in a book he had yet to read. He could no longer distinguish between the real and unreal, not from the first arrival of his madness until the moment of his death. I never met his wife, but I can only assume that this changed her tune.

But what of me? I left the service and met your mother. We fell in love immediately. The first night, I was hungrier for her than I had ever been for anything in my life. I hope you do not blush to read this, my dear daughter. I wish that one day you will find a man with as great an appetite for you. Nine months later, you were born and your mother died. I do not know a more elegant way to describe this turn of events. My sorrow raised you. I hope that it did not poison you.

I have come somewhat far from the history book. I am sorry, my dear, just as I am sorry that I only send you a letter once each year, on your birthday. Any more would put me in the ground, and I do not believe that you want me there. It is time for my letter to end now. As usual, I will close without a comma, with hope.

Love
your father

SEVENTEEN DIFFERENT WAYS TO GET A LOAD OF THAT

1.

From the air, the house looked like a joke told by someone with no sense of timing, a big brown rectangle in the middle of a slightly bigger green rectangle tatted with a white picket fence. The fence looked flimsy because the fence was flimsy. A child could knock it down, and did, several times, mostly as a result of trying to hurdle it and failing, sometimes just for spite. My father put up the fence when we moved in, to keep the dog in the yard. "Will you get a load of that?" said my mother, puffing on a cigarette. "Your father wants to prove that a lawyer can do more than lawyering. I'm pretty sure he can't." And sure enough, within three months, the dog—a small schnauzer beloved by my sister and my father, despised by my mother, and, for me, an object lesson in indifference—was gone through a corner of the fence where the slats flexed enough to permit its passage. "Where is Goosey?" Jill said, in a voice loaded up with tragic tones she had learned from the television. She did this all the time. It was difficult to take her seriously. "Where is my little dog Goosey?"

"I am so sorry," said my father. The grief in his voice was real.

2.

Since both my parents worked late, our dinners were prepared by a cook, a tall, thin woman named Catherine who was planning to open her own restaurant and who was, my mother told us, attempting to trick my father into becoming an angel. "That's a kind of investor," she said, as if there were any confusion. "I think he should think long and hard before he makes that kind of decision." She was one to talk. When my mother had been in charge of the cooking, dinner was a roll of the dice, both random and risky. We could have pizza four nights in a row, and then not see it again for a month. We could have fried chicken every other night for two months and then lose it for the better part of a year. It made for an unstable relationship with food. With Catherine, we entered into a regimen of strict rotation: chicken, pork, fish, pasta, beef. Each day of the week partnered with a certain entrée. "It's to help me learn what I need to know," Catherine said, her eyes glazing over as she drifted into thoughts of her future restaurant, which she was going to call the Hungry Cat. Fridays were for experiments; she tried tagines, pastry shells, exotic meats. One Friday, she served something she called "a Bull in the Grass," which consisted of a filet mignon served over a bed of spinach and topped with sautéed onions and mushrooms. Midway through the meal, I leaned over to Jill and said, "Why doesn't she call this 'a Goose in the Grass'?" My mother laughed. Jill burst into tears. My father said my name once sternly—it was also his own name—and then he said nothing. Had I not been so pleased with my own joke I might have noticed the way he stared at Catherine.

3.

My mother and Catherine didn't get along, and I wasn't sure why.

Certainly, my mother wasn't uncomfortable with the idea of having servants. She had grown up wealthy; her father was a prominent businessman back on Earth. Have I mentioned that we were no longer living on Earth? When gravity and oxygen were first introduced to the moon, the United States government arranged for the transfer of more than 25,000 Americans to Alpha Settlement. No one liked the name, so the government promised that after a year the residents could vote on a new name. That first year, while my parents were busy getting used to their new lives, meeting the neighbors, and fixing up the house—that was the year my father built the fence—Jill and I spent all our time thinking of names for Alpha Settlement.

As befits a self-serious fourteen-year-old, I favored dignified, slightly artificial names: Luna Village, Tranquility Hills. Jill, twelve, wanted a name that made her laugh: "Moonesota," she said, or "Moontana," or "Moonte Carlo." My mother and I indulged her names with weak smiles and encouraging nods. My father loved them. He was constantly asking Jill to think of new ones or, better yet, to make a list of all the ones she had thought of to date. One day he came home from work, and she rushed at him with open arms. "Daddy," she said. "I thought of three more today: Vermoont! Green Cheese City! Moonesota!" She was beginning to repeat herself, but normally that would have made no difference to my father. Normally, he would have stood next to her and laughed at each and every joke. This was not a normal day, though. He went to the dining room table, set down his briefcase, sat down stiffly, and told my sister and I that he was leaving my mother for Catherine.

4.

This was followed by a long explanation in which he touched on several subjects that were unfamiliar to me and Jill. He spoke about what he called "carnal and conversational compatibility," and did so in such a manner that it seemed he had not invented it, but rather had read about it somewhere. He warned us that when we picked a mate, we should be vigilant about ensuring that our moral compasses were oriented in the same direction. He even raised the issue of location: he had begun to feel strange since coming to the moon, he said, and worried that it was not natural to live there, no matter what the government said. When he was done with the speech, both Jill and I were thoroughly persuaded, and he sensed this. He nodded at us crisply, picked up his brief-case, and walked out of the kitchen. Jill and I rushed to the front window and watched him go through the gate in the fence. He closed it delicately and then he stood on the other side. He had one more short speech in him. "I put up this fence with my own hands," he said. "I intended for it to keep you safe, to keep us all safe. It did a poor job because I did a poor job. It let Goosey out and now it is letting me out. I hope it does a better job for you." He reached out to touch the gate, thought better of it, withdrew his hand. Then he turned and walked away. Jill began to cry. I kept staring out the window. Between the fence and the street, there were several hundred yards of empty frontage, which had two effects: first, to call into question the purpose of the fence; second, to allow me to watch my father recede slowly until he was no more than a tiny figure on the horizon of the evening. Then it was time for dinner, and I knew Catherine wouldn't be coming, so I ordered some pizza.

5.

My mother was out all afternoon, covering for a friend at the hospital where she worked as a physician's assistant, so she received confirmation of my father's departure by telegram that evening. The pizza was a halfer: cheese for Jill, who had declared herself a vegetarian since the Goose in the Grass incident, and sausage for me. My mother took a slice from each half and nibbled at them cautiously. Normally she liked pizza, but even before the telegram arrived, she had suspected that the dinner was a bad sign. The doorbell rang. A man in a white hat and white gloves was standing there, and there was an envelope in his hand. In some ways, Alpha Settlement, still young, was unnecessarily formal. My mother read the telegram several times to herself, put it on her plate, and slid the sausage slice over it as a form of burial. "He used to send me letters all the time," she said. And then she said no more. Had it been me, I would have closed my mouth if I had no more to say. But my mother did not close her mouth. In fact, she opened it wider, and then wider still. Jill and I, who had been staring down into the pizza, looked up at my mother's gaping mouth. We didn't know whether we were supposed to put something in there or take something out. Then my mother left the kitchen abruptly and went into her bedroom, where she stayed for one full month, occasionally emerging to shout at Jill or me, or drive to the liquor store, or watch old detective shows on TV. She loved to criticize the detectives when they missed obvious clues. "She's wearing different shoes than she was before the murder," she said. "Will you get a load of that?"

"He can't hear you," Jill said. "It's a TV." But my mother spoke with such volume that I wasn't sure that Jill was right.

6.

It would be nice to report that the love affair between Catherine and my father petered out—that she came to see him as an ineffectual man who had done his family wrong or that he came to see her as a siren who had tempted him into misdeed and mischance. In fact, his exit through the front door, and then the long pause by the fence, were the last we saw of him, at least in person. He married Catherine, moved back to Earth, helped her open the Hungry Cat, had a baby daughter named Rebecca, put ribbons in her hair, and developed a wide, toothy smile that he invariably displayed in the pictures that he sent us after birthdays and holidays. The photographs were accompanied by letters, and the letters, typed on a thin onionskin paper that allowed him to erase and retype over errors, were even more sadistic. He called Rebecca "your sister" and made outlandish promises to me and to Jill—vacations, ponies, battery-powered cars—that we believed painfully for the first year or two. The letters were addressed to me and to Jill at the house in Lunar City, for that was what Alpha Settlement had been named. Jill and I would sit in armchairs and read them, but my mother, aware that they represented a particularly efficient delivery mechanism for additional misery, seemed determined to ignore them. Every once in a while, though, she'd ask me or Jill how our father seemed to be doing. Jill scowled and refused to answer. "He seems a little unsure of himself, really," I said, gently.

7.

I was gentle to my mother because I loved her. Jill was rough with her because she loved my father more. I missed my father because his departure left me without an idea of the kind of man I might become at the same time that it forced me prematurely to become that man. Jill missed my father because she had been deprived of her first love. Perhaps these things are obvious, but they struck me as insights, particularly in those first few years after my father left.

I tried to raise the issue with Jill once when we were out in the yard fixing the fence. We were out there fixing it almost every week. She screwed up her face. "You talk so fancy out here," she said. "It's like the fence is making you think you're smarter. Do you think it can see inside the human soul? From now on I'm going to call it the Shrink Fence."

"Call it what you want," I said. "But don't deny how important it is to you to feel Dad's love."

"I'm not feeling anyone's anything," she said. "You're disgusting. Anyway, I don't love him. I hate him."

"You don't hate him," I said.

"Why would I love a man who walks out on his wife and children?" she said. "Why would I love a man who puts ribbons in that stupid little girl's stupid hair? Why would I love a man who let Goosey escape?"

Just a year before, this memory would have brought on tears, but Jill, now fourteen, was hardening quickly, and even Goosey was more a spur to anger than a source of sadness. "And on that same topic," she said, "why would I love a man who built this fence? Incompetent is the only way you can describe this thing." We had been packing in dirt around the bases of the fence-posts,

and now she stood and kicked at the post closest to her, and the
fence buckled like a bad idea and the section closest to her went
flat to the ground. Goosey wouldn't even have needed to squeeze
through the pickets. He could have just walked out, right over
them.

8.

My mother was as angry as Jill, if not more so, but she had a different style entirely. To the untrained eye, her anger probably
seemed as though it was pointing in all directions at once. It was
not, not by a long shot. She hated the government, particularly
the mayor, whom she held accountable for the way Lunar City
was zoned.

"It's his fault that we have almost no neighbors all the way
out here," she said. "I blame him for our loneliness." She hated
television detectives, as I have said, and pizza delivery boys, of
course. But that was about it. She loved nearly everyone else, and
she expressed that as passionately as she expressed her hatred.
When Jill turned fifteen, she started to date a pizza delivery boy
just to antagonize my mother, and she was always taunting her
by saying things like "We were there at the store late because it's
his job to lock up" or "I think I left my sweater in the back of his
van." Jill confessed to me that she didn't really like the guy, and
that she hadn't let him do more than put his hand up her shirt,
but that she was driven to get my mother's attention by at least
pretending to be committing these transgressions.

"Driven to get attention by committing transgressions," I
said. "Sounds like someone has been standing out by the Shrink
Fence."

"Whatever," Jill said. My mother was in the room now. "Anyway, I'm heading over to Eric's place. He has a new mattress."

My mother didn't take the bait. She never did where people she loved were concerned. "Bye, Sweetie," she said. "I can't see what you see in him, but I trust that if you see something, it's there. I believe in your judgment, because I feel that you are capable of great things. I hope you agree, or that you'll come to agree."

"Leaving," Jill said. "Leaving leaving leaving."

9.

But Jill didn't leave. I left. I worked hard in high school, happier in class than at home, and spent afternoons out by the fence, thinking things through. When it came time to apply to college, my mother pressured me to attend Lunar City University, which was a fine institution, staffed by some of the best minds in America, many of whom had jumped at the opportunity to teach on the moon, others of whom had been reluctant initially but found the large salaries persuasive. "What do you like, business?" my mother said. "You can study business there. They say on TV that lunar franchises are a big deal now. Lunar franchises: Will you get a load of that?"

"I don't like business," I said. "Not at all."

"What, then?" she said. "The law?" Her lip curled when she said it. But she loved me, and if I had said yes, she would have been right on it, weaving an elaborate defense of the law as a legitimate career.

"I don't know," I said. "I just want to go back to Earth." And so I did, to a nondescript four-year university in a nondescript state in the broad middle of the nation, only fifty miles or so from where my father had settled with Catherine and Rebecca. At first, my mother and I spoke on the phone every week, but the conversations grew strained. There was something in the extreme long distance of the call that diluted the tone of our voices and made each of us less liable to believe the other. For example, she suspected that I was secretly spending time with my father and Catherine there on Earth, though I told her plainly that I wasn't. And I suspected that she was angry at me, though that seemed impossible. One day, near the end of the first semester, she was worrying about what she should cook when I came back for vacation. I told her that I wasn't sure I was coming, that I was thinking of spending the holiday in Maine with a roommate. "It might be easier if you and Jill just ordered something," I said. I didn't mean anything by it, though I realized as I said it that it meant everything. My mother didn't speak for a few seconds. I imagined that her mouth was wide open. Then she told me that I was acting just like my father, which I took as a sign not to call her for a while.

10.

My relationship with Jill was better. We didn't talk on the telephone or send each other electronic messages. Instead, we exchanged letters, and in those letters she was able to give a fuller account of how she was feeling. In fact, they seemed to encourage her to try to understand her own motives and the motives of those around her, and to analyze before she judged; they were like a portable version of the Shrink Fence. At the start of my sophomore year in college, she visited me. By then, she was a swan of a young woman, tall and beautiful and capable of cool irony along with the silliness and surliness that were her trademarks. At least two of my friends fell in love with her during the week she was on campus, and one of them went so far as to spend his winter break working on the moon, calling her daily and offering to take her to expensive restaurants. He returned to college in the spring, defeated because Jill had spurned his advances. In the next letter she sent me, she explained. "It wasn't that there was anything wrong with Anton," she said. "But I met a guy here and I think I'm in love. He's a pizza delivery boy. Ha ha. I am just joking. But you know the irony of it? He owns the pizza store. His name is Jack Holland, and he moved up here from Earth just last year. He is a quite a bit older than me and divorced. He is also the tallest man in town, I think. He's six-eight if he's an inch. On our first date I told him about Moonesota and he laughed so hard he fell out of his chair. This is not an exaggeration or colorful language. He fell out of his chair. Sitting there on the ground, he was almost as tall as I was."

11.

In that same letter, Jill told me another piece of information, which was that my father had stopped writing her. This surprised me because I hadn't received any letters from him since I started college, and I had assumed that he wasn't writing to anyone. "I got them at a regular clip until last month," Jill wrote, "and then they stopped suddenly. I had come to depend on them, even though they were growing steadily more boring. A few months ago, he and Catherine took Rebecca to the zoo and then let her nap in the back office at the Hungry Cat while Catherine chalked the specials on the board. I know this because it's exactly what his letter said. It was so boring that even writing about it is boring. But it was a piece of him. I would like it if you would investigate and find out why he stopped writing. If you don't want to do it for me, do it for Mom. I'm pretty sure she has noticed that the letters have stopped, and I'm pretty sure that it bothers her. She grew accustomed to seeing them piling up in our rooms. It comforted her, if you can believe it." I folded up Jill's letter and slid it to the side of my desk.

Anton came by a minute later, saw the handwriting, and pulled up a chair. "If there's any way you'd give me another chance," he said. "I'll do anything."

"She can't hear you," I said. "It's a letter."

12.

I made some calls and read some articles and was able to find out more news about my father. He had gone on a business trip to the Pacific Rim, during which time he had contracted a bacterial infection from shellfish. He recovered from the infection, but it left him weak, and when he returned to the States, he was unable to climb the stairs to his office, even though it was only on the second floor. He took the elevator, and as he was impatient, he pressed the CLOSE DOOR button repeatedly. I mention the CLOSE DOOR button because it was the last button he ever pushed; the elevator panel had been removed and replaced, and the tongue end of a live wire had somehow been connected to the metal plate. The numbered buttons, the ones that instructed the elevator to travel to specific floors, were rimmed in rubber and consequently grounded. The OPEN DOOR and CLOSE DOOR buttons were not. Electricity pierced the tip of my father's finger. A blue flame traced the outline of his hand. Current ran around his heart, which chased the current until it was exhausted and collapsed. The newspaper account I read mentioned a possible lawsuit. It also mentioned that he was survived by his wife Catherine and his daughter Rebecca. I omitted this bit of information when I wrote to Jill with the news. She called me immediately when she received the letter. She was crying. "I need to go talk to Jack," she said, and her crying tapered off a bit.

13.

I kept writing letters to Jill. I thought she needed to receive them, and I knew that I needed to send them. Increasingly, though, she responded to my letters with phone calls. I tried to explain to her why this was a mistake, but she wouldn't listen. As a result of whatever she thought she was feeling with Jack, she was in the mind of doing something new—new for herself, new for the world—and that meant pushing past what I now saw she believed was an antiquated practice. It hurt me at first. We entered a brief period of opposition, which came as a shock to me, not because it arrived with any particular violence but because it arrived at all. It had been a long time since we had allowed ourselves to be enemies. The memory that came back to me most vividly during that time was the moment when I told her that we were eating Goosey; I was wrong to fix on it, of course, but I must have believed that it triggered the entire process that led my father to notice Catherine, to leave the house, to tie a ribbon in Rebecca's hair, to press the CLOSE DOOR button. For a week or so, I dropped into a deep depression, and my only consolation came from the fact that it was so theatrical that I knew it would not last. Then I met a girl who came from a town very near to where my father had lived, and then Anton started dating her friend, and I was all at once in a new thing of my own. I called Jill when I wanted to talk to her, and though this felt like a concession, it also felt like progress. The only persistent negative effect of the calls was that they brought into sharp relief the fact that I was still not talking to my mother. It had been nearly a year, and she had not asked for me, and I had not asked for her. She would watch as my sister spoke to me, but we were both too proud to end the silence. When Jill told me that she was starting to fail a bit, that she would sometimes forget Jill's name or insist that my father was just late coming home from work, it should have encouraged me to call directly, but it had the opposite effect. I had broken off talking to my mother while she was still vibrating with hatred for my father and the mayor and love for everyone else. I did not want to find her again only to discover that she had been diminished.

14.

One day, out walking in a neighborhood near campus, I had a very clear vision of the house where I grew up, as seen from overhead: the brown rectangle, the green rectangle, the white fence. In my vision, my mother was there, standing forlornly in a corner of the front lawn, and I suddenly came over with an idea. Since I could no longer write letters to Jill, and since I could no longer speak to my mother on the phone, I would write letters to my mother.

The first one was written with the kind of unthinking innocence that always reveals itself, in time, to be a form of deceit. I decided to type it because my mother had always complained that she could not read my handwriting. I obtained onionskin paper because it was the best lightweight paper available at the campus bookstore. (Perhaps the Shrink Fence would challenge both of these statements.) In that first letter, I affected a more adult tone because I wanted to impress her with my independence. "I know we haven't spoken for a while," I wrote. "I wish it weren't the case. Life in the States is good." The rest of it was small talk about the news, save for one long sentence at the end where I tried to communicate what I understood of human connection: "The way in which I faded away is unforgivable and I would not blame you if you agreed," I wrote, "which is why I am not asking that you write back, only that you continue to let me write to you." I was helping my girlfriend move some furniture at her parents' house that weekend, and I deposited the letter virtuously in a box at the corner of the street.

A few days later, my mother called me. "Guess what?" she said. "Your father wrote me a letter."

15.

The monstrosity of this misunderstanding should have compelled me to clarify matters right then and there. Why I didn't, I will never know. But rather than disabuse my mother of her delusion, I redoubled it. I sent another letter, and this time I clearly took on my father's persona, right down to the easy eloquence he assumed when painful matters were close at hand. "So much time," he wrote, "and so little time within that time to make amends. Going backward, well, that is the behavior of a fool, but going forward without acknowledging the ways in which I crippled the past so that it could only hobble into the present, that is the behavior of a villain." When I mailed that second letter, I was sure that I would be found out, if not by my mother, then by Jill. But Jill was out of the house, and my mother was failing, and this letter was something that she believed in more completely than if it were true. On the phone, she told me that he had written her again. "He moved to the earth," she said, as if she had forgotten that I lived there, too. She was calling me regularly now, in part because she was rejuvenated by the letters, and in part because she was aging rapidly and forgot the calls almost as soon as she made them.

I should have stopped after two letters, or three, or five, or ten.

16.

When Jill decided to marry Jack Holland, there was no thinking long and hard. She just did it, stepped into a bone-white cocktail dress and drove herself to a justice of the peace on the other side of town. Jack came straight from the pizza shop to meet her there. I didn't think he was right for her, and it had nothing to do with the fact that she was only eighteen. He was too powerful, too big, with reserves of rough strength it seemed unlikely that she would be able to control. She was a delicate person, no matter how much she liked to pretend otherwise.

I didn't tell her that. Instead, I congratulated her and asked her if there would be a party to celebrate. "Mom said she'll throw one, but she's slipping further every day," Jill said. "I think I'll have one for myself. But you have to promise to come and to bring your girlfriend."

"Where will it be?"

"At the house, of course," she said. Her voice had an offended note in it.

My girlfriend had never been to the moon, and I overprepared her with stories about everything I could remember. Our flight was delayed, and we arrived midway through the party. As I came across the frontage, I saw that there were balloons tied to the fence. It looked like they were holding it up. I opened the gate gingerly and motioned my girlfriend through. Jill was the first person I saw, and her new husband was the second. I hugged her and shook his hand and told them both that, for the first time in my life, I felt certain that I didn't have to worry about my sister. Behind them was a long wide table loaded with pizza. "Very nostalgic," I said to Jill.

"What do you mean?" Jack said thuddingly. "I brought the food."

"You did," Jill said, and pulled him close to her. He refused to bend, and he towered over her, but he looked down with an expression that had no condescension, no cruelty, and no pity. It was an expression of total and unconditional devotion, and it came through loud and clear.

17.

Jill and I stood in a corner of the yard while Jack took my girlfriend on a tour of the house. We made the smallest small talk: when I thought I might graduate, where she and Jack would live. Two little boys and a dog were playing tag outside of the fence. One boy lunged for the other, who evaded the tag. He bumped into the fencepost closest to us, which pulled up slightly.

"Someone should fix that," Jill said.

"I'll get right on it," I said.

"You should see Mom," Jill said.

"Of course," I said. "Do you think I forgot?" But the truth was that I had.

My mother was sitting up against the house, in an armchair someone had brought out to the lawn. She was a small brown husk, hardly recognizable. But she brightened immediately when she saw me. "Is this your girlfriend?" she said, pointing at Jill. She grasped Jill's hand. "You're an angel," she said. "I hope Goosey isn't bothering you. He's a horrible little thing."

Jill scowled, then remembered who she was supposed to be. She smiled and excused herself. "I'm going to go powder my nose," she said.

My mother took me by the elbow and pulled me down close to her mouth.

"You know who I've been hearing from?" she said.

"No," I said.

"Your father," she said. "I didn't tell you before because I didn't want to upset you. I know that he stopped writing to you a while ago." She paused, gripped the arms of her chair as if she might stand, thought better of it, relaxed. "Letters from your father," she said. "Will you get a load of that?"

"I am so sorry," I said. The grief in my voice was real.

DOWN A POUND

SHE HATES THE WAY HE WEIGHS HIMSELF EACH DAY. SHE HAS turned this into a kind of jingle. "She hates the way / He weighs himself / Each day." It has the same melody as a commercial on television for a local car-repair shop. The repair shop's song is "When something breaks / Just take your car / To Lake's." Sophie is thinking about the repair shop jingle while she drives along. Something has been rattling in the corners of the dash-board. Joe rarely rides in her car, and he won't let her drive his truck, so the noise is her problem. "I'll take a look at it," he had said the night before, without a shred of conviction. Then he went into the bathroom to weigh himself.

He thinks that she doesn't notice that he's vain about his weight. She does notice, because when she was younger, she had a close friend named Peter who always used to complain about men who weighed themselves. "A man should only know what he weighs within five pounds," Peter said. "And if he lies about his weight, he should lie on the high side. Being a man is about being a mass, at least in part." Peter communicated his theories to her in rambling monologues that he wrote up longhand and sent as if they were love letters, which she supposed they were. He was uncertain about some of his theories, like the one about the faked moon landing or the one about feline telepathy. But he was sure about men and weight. "Look at me," Peter said. "I'm two-twenty. You don't hear me crying about my weight." Peter was one-ninety, tops. She took his point.

Joe was two-twenty, most days. That morning he had come out of the bathroom with a smile on his face. "Down a pound," he had said. Sophie was still in bed. She smiled back at his smile without thinking about why she was doing it. Since Joe had started weighing himself incessantly, Sophie had stopped weighing herself. There was some advantage to his compulsion and his weakness. Maybe that's why she was smiling back at him.

Back when she was friends with Peter, he had wanted to date her, which was not something he had ever expressed in his letters. The implication was there, but he worked the edges and the margins, waited until they were together, at a movie, and just as it started, he touched her arm. "I want to be with you, you know," he said. Peter was a very aggressive man, but when he told her that he wanted to date, he did not sound very aggressive. He sounded like he was holding an eggshell in his hand. During the movie, his hand dangled over the armrest and brushed against her thigh with a heartbreaking timidity. Sophie waited until the movie was over, and then she said no to Peter. She told him that he was just a friend, that she could not imagine them in a more romantic relationship. That was a lie. She imagined it often, and most of the times her imagination carried her through to a time when Peter would recognize that he did not care about her as much as he thought he did. Under the influence of that new epiphany, he would slowly drift away, or run off with another woman, and Sophie would be left behind to feel hollow or, more precisely, filled with nothing. That was her thinking as she told him no. He looked at her without blinking, then blinked, and that blink returned everything to normal, such as it was. The next day he sent her a letter in which he told her that plastic was a living organism hell-bent on populating the planet to the point where it crowded out all other species. "Frogs, toads, all," he wrote, in large looping letters.

Joe has said that if Sophie ever left him, he would feel bereft. Joe does not know what the word means. Joe has also apologized for being aggressive. He does not know what that word means either. In fact, one of the reasons he was selected over someone like Peter was that he was not very aggressive. He was selected? She is removing herself from the equation even when she is the subject of the sentence. She hits herself with a nun's ruler, mentally.

Sophie does not worry about Joe leaving her. Joe is not the kind of guy who leaves. He has told her that repeatedly. The night before, at dinner, after his third glass of wine, he bumped his knees against the table and said it again. "Once I was the kind of man who would leave," he said, "but you cured me." She put her hand out on the table, and he rolled his hand on top of it. "I feel full," he said. "Like this bottle." He tapped the wine bottle, which wasn't near full anymore. He was too drunk to drive, so she slid into the driver's seat and piloted his truck home. "We have to fix that rattling in your car," Joe said, "but the last time that mechanic jobbed me for twenty percent more than it should have cost. Is there such a thing as an honest body shop? It's good those guys aren't doctors. You could be spread out on the hospital bed, just laid out, and the last thing you'd see was the dollar signs in their eyes." He was still talking when they went to bed—this time, about an idea he had for a special kind of mailbox that would separate bills from the rest of the mail. They had sex, which stopped him talking. He buried his face in the pillow next to her head when he came. And then he was asleep, just like that.

When Sophie first came to America, she was twelve. Her father stayed in France with his new wife, who had been his girl-friend throughout the marriage to her mother. She was a black woman, American, everything her mother was not, and because of that her mother endured the infidelity, even the fact that when Sophie was four, her father had gotten the other woman preg-nant. "He's a musician," her mother said, as if that explained ev-erything. But then the other woman leaned on Sophie's father for a wedding, and that was too much for her mother, and they came to America. Her mother worked two jobs, at a coffee shop and a copy shop. Given her accent, it was hard to tell the difference. Add to that the fact that they were one right next to the other, in a little strip mall. That was comedy. That's where they lived, in an apartment building on the Near North Side of Chicago. Every-thing was within walking distance: her mother's jobs, her school. Sophie slept in a narrow little room without a window. In the evenings and mornings her mother used to stand in the doorway and announce the time. "I am the sun and the moon," she said. Eventually the sun and the moon took a job as a secretary in the art department at a local university. This proved to be a brilliant stroke, as it ensured that Sophie had a substantial tuition credit for her own studies. All she needed to do was drop by twice a week and take her mother to lunch. She did not mind. She loved her mother even if it bothered her that her mother refused to eat anything more than a small salad and a side of buttered bread. "These aren't wartime conditions," Sophie said. "And yet we are not at peace," her mother said, with the mixture of twinkling

irony and dead seriousness that Sophie recognized as a sign of
pain processed in such a way that it did not become poisonous—
or, as she preferred to call it, of intelligence.

Sophie did well in college, applied herself to studies rather
than to boys or to art, though she was talented in those areas as
well. She got work as a paralegal and was soon the head paralegal
at a large firm. She always meant to go back to law school, but she
had to take care of her mother, who was getting older and was
sometimes in poor health. It seemed like the wrong time. Also,
something tugged at her. She didn't want to rise too far above her
station, which was exactly 2.8 notches above her mother's station.
If her mother had been a lawyer, she would have been a more successful lawyer. If her mother had been a failure, that would have
given her freedom. In her mind she marks off the distance from
her mother. In her mind she marks off the distance from everyone. It's what her mind is for.

Her mother knows this, though Sophie has never explained
it. Her mother hates it. The week before, she had gone to sit with
her mother. "I do not want you to calculate on me," her mother
said. "You are a strange child. You do so much for me that changes
your own life, but when you sit here with me, you are cold like
a decaying porgy." It was something her mother had read and
she clearly did not understand it, but she spoke with conviction.
Peter had not liked her mother. "She is always so sure of herself,"
he said. "Should a woman be that sure of herself?"

"What are some of the other choices?" Sophie said.

Peter did not quite laugh at her joke. Men were forever not
quite laughing at her jokes. The night before, when Joe had told
her that he felt like a full bottle, she had made another joke. Joe
was asleep, or nearly asleep. "You're the bottle," she said to his
motionless form. "Right? Well, sometimes I feel like the cork that

goes down with the rest of the bottle when it's tossed in the water." He didn't disagree, but he didn't laugh either.

Joe was definitely asleep. Maybe that's why he hadn't laughed.
She gave him the benefit of the doubt. Joe slept so soundly that
he liked to call himself the decedent. He laughed at his own joke
whenever he said that. Sophie could not sleep. She had a job that
required her to lay awake for long hours retracing her steps, and
nothing seemed to help. Sex did not put her to sleep but rather
put her in a state of heightened awareness. While she was having sex with Joe, she found herself looking up into his face as he
chugged along and wondering how it had come to this. His was
the face of a child, shot through with a tragic lack of understanding of its own mortality. It was not the face of a man. Not really.
She reached up and brushed his cheek and he mistook her touch
for tenderness.

With Joe asleep, she found herself thinking of sex. What was
it, exactly? What was pleasure? Had she felt it? Something had
seemed to widen in the space behind her nose, to enlarge her, but
was that pleasure? How would she know, exactly? Joe had put a
finger inside her. What was he pointing at? What was that rivulet
of fluid growing cold on her thigh? Was it her blood? And what
was the point of Joe's weight on her, exactly? Was he making a
point about his bulk? Was he trying to remind her of his physical
power? It was unlikely. He was not aggressive. Sex kept her up,
thinking.

Her bed, too, kept her up. It was not comfortable. Something
in the sheets gave her cause to itch. A bed should not be like
that. If it was not a place of peace, then where was peace? She
listened to the blood beat in her ears. Who else was awake? Her
mother, probably. Her mother had never slept easily either. She
was too often lonely, or afraid, or angry. Maybe sleep, or the lack

of sleep, passed like knowledge or sadness from mother to daughter. Maybe all of this was her mother's fault. She watched the time on the clock creep along and cursed her mother, her bed, her life. She cursed Joe. She cursed sex. She looked out the window and cursed the night sky. "If I never see you again," she said to the moon, "it'll be too soon." She closed her eyes and thought of ways of changing things for the better. She must have fallen asleep eventually, because she remembered dreaming, though she did not remember any details of the dream. She called her mother in the morning to arrange a visit. "I love you," she said to her mother.

"Will you bring Joe?" her mother said.

"Yes," Sophie said.

"Well, it's up to you," her mother said. No one's tone was convincing.

JOE LOVED HER MOTHER. He had an easy way with her. He told her jokes and she laughed. He got her drinks and she said thank you. Sophie resented this, not because she wanted there to be tension between them but because she knew that Joe was not touching her mother's core. That core was a hot thing—hot and cold both, to be precise—and when it was touched in any way the result was discomfort for everyone. Joe kept her mother comfortable and he was comfortable in return. He smiled at everything she said, even when what she said was sharp or uneasy. He ate whatever she put in front of him, even though Sophie knew that later on in bed he would turn from his back to his side and sigh in a way that let her know he was worrying about his weight. If asked, he would say nothing bad about her mother. "I like going over there," he'd say. "It's a nice place." And just like that, she was left to stay awake in the bed, where the corners of the mattress rose up slightly, where the equatorial bar bruised her back and shoulders.

That's where she's going this afternoon: to see her mother and then buy a new bed. She told Joe that she was going to the drugstore. This struck her as an acceptable lie. She didn't want to get into a discussion with him about the bed, and whether it should be replaced, and what implications that would have for their relationship and the future of the planet. She just wanted to sleep. Joe seems to be sleeping more than ever. For more than a week he has been slack, like a clothesline strung indifferently between two buildings. The preoccupation with his weight is only part of it. He has been listless. He has started to drink too much again. He has complained that he does not know what he wants from life, that he cannot imagine going forward while he is in the grip of this inertia. "But inertia is what makes you go forward," she says. They were both right, but she was more right.

The radio is playing Billie Holiday, a song called "You Go to My Head." Sophie knows the song, knows it well. Here, credit is due not her mother but her father. He plays the trumpet, sometimes professionally, and when she was a baby he had been obsessed with American singers. A truck goes by with a picture of a ghost on the side, which reminds her of a line in the song: "Though I'm certain that this heart of mine hasn't a ghost of a chance in this crazy romance, you go to my head." She and Joe do not listen to music together very often. Mostly it's in the car. A radio is never on as they are going to bed or waking up. When she was friends with Peter, they used to listen to music all the time. Peter was obsessed with Smokey Robinson. "These songs tell you who to love," he used to say. "Whoever you think of while you are listening to these songs, well, that is who you love." When

Peter explained this theory, Sophie saw how brightly hope was burning in his eyes. She could not endorse that hope. Instead, she fell silent and stayed that way.

At the time that Peter had asked Sophie to date him and Sophie had refused, she had told Peter she was sorry, and while it was a lie, it was also a prediction, because that time did eventually come. She thought of him often and was sorry when she did. Now in the car, as she drives to her mother's house, she wonders where Peter is. He lingers like a haunting refrain. The song ends. Next is another Billie Holiday song, "They Can't Take That Away from Me." Sophie sings along. "The memory of all that, no, no, they can't take that away from me." She imagines her mother's voice next. This is becoming quite a play. "Oh, but they can take that away," she hears her mother say. "Can and will. So be careful." Her mother loves Joe. He is often the first thing she asks about. "It is so important to pick the right man to marry," she tells Sophie. When her mother speaks of Joe, she rarely has any irony in her tone.

Her mother picked the wrong man to marry. He had run around, had a child with another woman, and eventually left. And it wasn't as though there was no proof of his error: his daughter by the second wife lived in America now, although everyone said she was crazy. These were some very real consequences, her mother said, and every chance she got, she told Sophie not to repeat her mistake. Sometimes she even made her voice quaver when she said it, so she sounded like a ghost. "Dooooo not doooo what I have donnnnne," she said. Again, the pain processed in such a way that it did not become poisonous. The memory of her mother's ghost voice makes Sophie smile, although she feels a soft thud in her heart at the thought that perhaps the crime has already been committed. The last days have been criminal at many points. She was not able to look at Joe directly during dinner. She was angry at him in the truck. She disparaged him silently while he weighed himself. This is not the way it should be. Joe is kind. Joe will never leave. Joe will eventually fix the car. In "My Man," Billie Holiday's lover beat her up and ran around and still couldn't weaken her devotion. That's not Joe, not at all.

Joe would be surprised to learn that Sophie knows nearly every song Billie Holiday ever recorded. She knows "Riffin' the Scotch" and "With Thee I Swing" and "Spreadin' Rhythm Around" and "That's Life I Guess." Joe thinks that she does not know very much about music because she is young. He takes a squinty view of both her facts and her opinions. The night before, in the truck, there was a song that he loved and she didn't. "I don't know it or care to know it," she said. He sniffed and said, "You always have a bone to pick musically." Sophie was offended. She marked off the distance from Joe in her mind. But now, as she drives, she decides that she loves the sound of what Joe said. She feels like she has been recognized as the virtuoso of some rare instrument. That is what angels should play instead of harps: a bone. She likes the image so much that it relieves the pain of the insult almost entirely.

She drives by the exit she would take if she were going to her office. She has a job that requires her to sit at a desk and decide the fates of others. She would rather sit in her mother's house, eat some food, have a drink, and talk about her own fate. Her mother never forgets to ask. "And what will happen next?" she likes to say to Sophie. From another mother to another daughter, this could be an overbearing question. But Sophie's mother does not have an answer in mind. "Sometimes the second step is distant from the first," she likes to say, waving her hand. What will happen next? It is worth thinking about.

The exit to her office sets her thinking about work. The day before had been the Friday before a Monday that will contain her biggest meeting in months. The Monday meeting was the main reason she could not sleep, even after sex. Her firm is fighting an injunction that would halt construction on a large office park in a subdivision called Potter Grove. The advocates who have filed the injunction are arguing that the construction would most likely pollute a nearby aquifer. The lawyers in her office are trying to get a judge to lift the injunction by arguing that one of the other attorneys is out of jurisdiction, and tracing that attorney's history has fallen to Sophie and her staff of paralegals. Every detail has to be in place. When, that morning, Joe had started complaining that he did not feel motivated in his own life, that he felt as though he were stalling, she had given him a hug when what she really wanted to do was to push him against the wall. While she hugged him, she noticed that it was harder than ever to reach all the way around him. Maybe he had gained weight. She marked off the distance from him. What would happen next?

Suddenly she remembers the dream she had the night before, when she was stretched out alongside Joe, wondering if she would ever sleep again, backtracking over the sex that had just concluded. At some point, she had answered most of her questions or decided that they could not be answered, and she had remembered that there was at least a little pleasure in it for her. She had squeezed her hand between her legs and then relaxed into sleep, where she had dreamed about Peter. He was a judge, and he was presiding over her life. He was deciding which man deserved her, and what music she should listen to, and whether she needed to work fourteen-hour days, and whether she should have a child. He made his opinions known in writing, behind elaborate wax seals. She was angry at first, and then relieved. Why not put your future in the hands of someone you trust? Toward the end of the dream, issues of jurisdiction returned, but they were blurry.

She is tired in the car. She has been tired all morning. She has never been more tired. While she was making coffee, she had almost put her hand in the machine. Joe does not know she is tired. How would he? The rattling noise, which is usually annoying, is putting her to sleep. In the car she has another kind of dream. It lasts only a second, and then she is back awake, worried that she has missed the turnoff for her mother's house. The radio isn't playing Billie Holiday anymore. It's playing Smokey Robinson. The song is called "Swept for You Baby," and though she does not remember ever hearing it before, she finds herself singing along. She makes a mental note to tell Peter, and then another mental note that she does not tell Peter anything anymore. It is nothing she can tell Joe. Maybe she will tell her mother. The rattling noise is putting her to sleep again. The sun is in her eyes. Her back itches and she resolves to scratch it the next time the car comes to rest at a stop sign or a red light.

The next time the car comes to rest, it is not at a stop sign or a red light. What are some of the other choices? It is overturned. Sophie is out on the road under the hood. Inertia has brought her there. Broken glass is spread around like rhythm. A bone comes through her arm. An artery in her thigh is laid open for all the world to see. "Look at my blood!" she wants to say. It is healthy blood, and it is running out. Time is running out with it. She is growing lighter than air. She has a sudden urge to weigh herself.

THE GOVINDAN ANANTHANARAYANAN ACADEMY FOR MORAL AND ETHICAL PRACTICE AND THE TREATMENT OF SADNESS RESULTING FROM THE MISAPPLICATION OF THE ABOVE

THE ACADEMY LASTED ONLY A DECADE, THOUGH THE BUILD-ing that housed it, a former boomerang factory, still stands on the border between India and Australia. It is a modest edi-fice, low and long, built in 1912 by the firm of Eyre and Anan-thanarayanan, which is today best known for its construction of warehouses throughout Asia but which was at the time inter-ested primarily in erecting a structure for the manufacture of the company's flagship product. Sections of the factory were rebuilt several times during its first decade, but the façade has been preserved unaltered since 1920. It is a distinctive façade. There is one window shaped like a boomerang and another shaped like the head of Markandeya, and midway between them a large iron door, above which is inscribed the official slogan of the Kaybee

Karmic Boomerang Company, "We'll keep you coming back for more," which was coined by Andrew Eyre, the son of one of the founders, in 1914. Above the door on the inside are two signs, one above the other, that were installed soon after. The top sign bears a picture of a piglike man surrounded by what looks like fire. No one understands that sign. Below that, there is a sign that says, "How do you feel when the person who made you the saddest feels sad?" This same question appeared, printed on a small laminated card, in selected boxes of the company's first shipment of Karmic Boomerangs, which were sent to toy stores and Hindu bookstores. Other questions in the series included "When a thief is robbed, should you laugh or cry?" and "How long must the good man wait for his lifetime good deeds to redound to him?" Govindan Ananthanarayanan, also the son of one of the founders, composed eight of these questions in all, and affixed one to the longer arm of each Karmic Boomerang. The question above the factory door was his favorite of them. It was the one he kept coming back to—"as you might expect," he joked, to the very mild amusement of his family and colleagues—and for that reason he had it turned it into a sign.

The question was interesting to Govindan mainly because he could not answer it. Karmic Boomerangs, which sold slowly at first, became, in the middle years of the decade, a huge hit in both Sydney and Bombay. You could see them everywhere in public meadows and beaches. One writer noted that "these chevrons of virtue fill the sky like a child's drawings of birds fill a child's drawings." Their vogue was short-lived, however. They were considered novelties, though Govindan Ananthanarayanan insisted that they were in fact "functioning ethical devices," and as quickly as they rose to prominence they fell away into obscurity. Both of Kaybee's founding families had made small fortunes with the ethical boomerang by then, and while the Eyres went on to become tycoons in the construction industry—taking with them the Eyre and Ananthanarayanan name, which allowed them to do business in India as well as Australia—the Ananthanarayanans, and particularly Govindan, embarked on a more scholarly course. This was not entirely surprising. Before Govindan had composed the eight questions that were packaged with the Karmic Boomerang, he had briefly attended Oxford University, where he had begun to assemble research for a thesis on James Harris Fairchild. Whether Govindan was inspired directly by his father's company's boomerang has been lost to history, but what is known is that following the conversion of the company to a construction firm, he reopened the factory as an academy of ethics. Initially, the curriculum was restricted to only nine courses, eight of which were based on the questions from the Kaybee cards. (The ninth was a late addition entitled "Should you ever lie to a man who tells you that he has always told the truth, but whom you suspect of untruth?") Govindan himself taught "How do you feel when the person who made you the saddest feels sad?"

Govindan's course notes no longer exist, and as enrollment was extremely limited in those early years, we do not have any extant accounts from the perspective of students. We do, however, have a letter that Govindan wrote to a friend of his, a man named James Rouse, that deals with this same set of questions. A small amount of background is necessary. Govindan was a married man. He had, like so many young Indians, consented to an arranged marriage; his bride to be was Prabhavati Priyadarshini, a young woman whose parents were friends of the Ananthanarayanans. The wedding took place in 1922, and accounts of it suggest that it was generally happy. Three years earlier, though, when Govindan was first informed of the match, he rebelled, insistent that he be allowed to find his own partner. Shortly after, in the summer of 1920, while studying once again at Oxford, he took notice of a young Englishwoman, Louisa Pelham. She was nineteen at the time. Govindan and Louisa embarked on a short and rocky romance that summer, and when he returned to Bombay that fall, he announced to his father that he would not marry Priyadarshini. The family refused to recognize Gonvindan's refusal. The next summer, Govindan returned to Oxford, only to find that Louisa had agreed to marry another man. Throughout that winter, he expressed his suffering in a series of letters to Rouse, an Englishman he had befriended who was also close friends with Andrew Eyre. Most of the letters between Govindan and Rouse have been lost. This letter survives: in it, Govindan reacts to the news that Louisa's marriage is an unhappy one, and addresses the same question that would become the focus of his course at the academy.

Dear Jim,

I received a letter from Louisa last week in which she was entirely despondent. Now and again a line would be smudged as a result of what I assume were her tears falling onto the page. The reasons, as I know you know, have to do with her marriage to Bartlett, and his treatment of her, which I am sure that you would call "beastly." I can see you saying that precise word and shaking your head uncomprehendingly. Your failure to understand human cruelty is one of the most worthy things about you.

I have, though, a separate issue to confront. As I am sure you remember, Louisa, after taking me higher than a woman has any right to take a man, brought me lower than I thought I could go in this lifetime. It felt like I would have to ascend at least a few levels just to reach the sadness of death. It was hardly malicious on her part—after all, I was arranged to marry another woman—but it still, at the time, felt like I had been run through with a sword.

Last week, when I received her letter, and discovered within a few sentences that she was writing from a place of great sadness, I wondered how I should feel. I mean this exactly as I have said it. I did not know how to feel. We all know about the German notion of Schadenfreude, or the Scots Gaelic aighear millteach, or the Hungarian káröröm, but those define a class of reactions to the general sufferings of others. Here, I am wondering about how to react to the sadness of those who cause you sadness. I would have thought there was something in Louisa's letter that would give me, at least for a moment, a kind of joy. She had spurned me, in a sense, and the choice she made elsewhere had turned out to be a bad one. Some would say it serves her right. But then I started thinking of the times that I would sit with her in the garden, or take walks with her, and the light that would stream from her eyes as she described the type of woman she wished to become in the world. The more vividly I remembered her presence, the more crushed I was to think that any part of that light had been extinguished by fear, exhaustion, or a sense of failure. It would be melodramatic to say that I cried her tears, but inaccurate to claim that they did not at least sting my eyes and make them water.

And yet, there is a countermovement. Does she want my sadness? Is there not some danger of her feeling it as pity, or as an attempt to regain the power and control I lost when she turned me out romantically? Perhaps I am not the right person to feel sad for her. Perhaps indifference, while impossible, would be more appropriate. I do not know exactly, Jim, but I welcome your thoughts on the matter.

Yours,
Govindan

Rouse's reply has survived.

My Dearest Govindan,

Your question is a hard one, which is why I am making no attempt to answer it.

My thoughts on the matter are the same as usual—I feel like fitting you for a priest's collar and then pulling it tight around your neck until you are dead. It would be a merciful act, my friend, as you have rarely shown even the slightest inclination toward existing in the moment or on this good green earth, where blood courses through bodies until it finds expression in unmentionable articulations. Your head is in the clouds, as they say, and clouds are in your head. Down here on the ground, we live not by ideas but by impulses and consequences. For my part, I recently put a bun in the oven of a lovely little Belgian nurse. She is carrying high and believes that it will be a boy. Can I trouble you for a few Karmic Boomerangs? They are no longer available at toy shops or Hindu bookstores here in London, but I think the little nipper would enjoy them.

Love to Prabhavati,

Jim

Rouse did not take delivery of the boomerangs. Only six months after this exchange, he arrived at the academy to assume the duties of grounds manager and rugby coach, which had previously been performed by Andrew Eyre, who had departed for America. Rouse came without his Belgian girlfriend or his son. A note that Eyre wrote to Govindan at that time elaborates on the circumstances that brought Rouse to the academy. It is significantly more telegraphic than the other men's letters: "Jim," Eyre writes, "ran. I understand. Found out that the child wasn't his, decided to stay and do his part. Passed through a change. Became a changed man. Then found out that the child was his after all. Some men would have been happy. Jim reasoned that any woman who would have been willing to have another man's child was—well, Jim ran. Hope he's good for rugby." In fact, during Rouse's time there, the institution earned far more renown for its athletics than it did for its moral and ethical instruction. The teams, whether in rugby or football, were extremely competitive, almost martial, and showed little mercy for their opponents. In fact, the marked contrast between the comportment of students in the classroom and on the field became central to the curriculum. One course dealing with the issue, taught by Govindan in 1929, was called "If you destroy an opponent, should you be eternally worried that your opponent will one day return to destroy you?"

The academy was shuttered in 1931, after a protracted lawsuit brought by the father of a former student who was injured during a rugby match; the suit held that Rouse's style of coaching led directly to the injury. All of the academy's remaining assets, including several dozen cases of boomerangs, were sold off to pay the settlement, as was the building itself, which became a community center and a museum dedicated to the history of the transcontinental border. Govindan, who had managed not to lose any of his personal wealth, moved to Sydney with his family—and Rouse, still single, came along. In Sydney, two months later, out walking along the waterfront and back, Govindan Ananthanarayanan encountered Louisa Pelham Bartlett, who had come to Australia after the death of her husband. The two of them resumed a friendship, and Govindan encouraged her to strike up a relationship with Rouse, who was occupying a small apartment in the back house of the Ananthanarayanan estate. "I know that this makes no sense to you, because it makes no sense to me," he wrote to

Eyre in 1933, "but I want to keep her near me, and I am hoping that if she takes up with Rouse it will achieve the desired effect. Desired effect: that is far too neutral and scientific a phrase for the almost childish joy I am hoping I might one day feel."

It was not to be. Rouse was, by this time, a hard man, impossible to reason with, let alone love, and his abrasive manner drove Pelham Bartlett away from the Ananthanarayanan family. More to the point, it drove her out of Australia; she soon married an American businessman, who then moved to Kyoto. Rouse insisted that Pelham Bartlett's departure did not bother him, as he had felt nothing for the woman when she was present. Nevertheless, he was keenly aware that his friend was suffering from her absence all over again, and this brought on a nervous breakdown that landed Rouse in Sacred Heart Hospital. "You didn't want her around anyway," Rouse wrote to Govindan from the hospital. "She had harmed you. Don't you remember? Why would you want to keep ties with someone like that? I must confess I don't understand you. But I am sorry if I have harmed you."

After six months, Rouse was released, and he returned to the Ananthanarayanan home, where he began to work as a driver for the family. When Rouse heard in 1940 that his former girlfriend had died in a car accident, he was at the horse track with Govindan Ananthanarayanan. "A driver killed her?" Rouse reportedly said. "That evens the score." He took off his driver's cap, placed it over his heart, and lowered his head. "My failure to understand human cruelty," he said, and began to laugh.

COUNTRY LIFE IS THE ONLY LIFE WORTH LIVING; COUNTRY LOVE IS THE ONLY LOVE WORTH GIVING

WE SET OFF FOR THE STATION THAT MORNING, LILY AND I. I know it pains you to hear this, my dear wife, but I feel I must tell the tale forward. You and I are one, in ways that we once discussed with regularity and even celebrated when you were my wife and I was your husband. Then we were divided. I am sorry, for I prefer love to war, but the truth is standing in the middle of the room and so I will not ignore it. The truth is your absence and Lily's presence. I say "presence" euphemistically, when what I mean is something more specific. She is standing here, her dress not quite covering it.

We had been living in the city together for a little less than a year, Lily and I. Most of our time was spent in an apartment, exercising one another and dreaming of the day when we might start again in a finer place. I hadn't known exactly what I meant by that, "a finer place," until the postman delivered a letter written to Lily by an elderly friend of her parents, one Mrs. Pritchard. This fine woman had heard from Lily's parents that Lily was looking for a place to spend part of the summer, and she was writing with a suggestion that took the form of a description of a village, and a road in it, and a house on that road that sounded like nothing so much as perfection. You and I once spent a summer in a village, but it was a dingy thing, with narrow paths that made movement through it nearly impossible. This village, as communicated by Mrs. Pritchard, sounded in me like a high note. Lily did not agree, but she did not have to; I heard her agreement in her silence.

At the train station on the morning of our departure, we were ringed by the denizens of the city that we had not, up until that very moment, met, and a more decrepit and disreputable crew I cannot imagine: There was a blind boy who could say only the words "more" and "money," a crippled girl who tried to stay faithful to her innocent girlhood but was betrayed by the voluptuous flowering of her figure, and a man with a maimed hand who looked at the girl with a rude hunger that left no doubt as to the eventual destination of the hand. The deformities, both of body and of soul, came out of every corner of the station, and they reminded me of the small cottage in the seaside town where you and I stayed on our honeymoon. That was our village, and it was tolerable only because we went there with a hope that protected us from its reality. Do you remember? There were noises in the walls as something scuttled from left to right and top to bottom, like a text we were afraid to read. That was how I expressed it at the time, and you laughed and said that was too beautiful a conceit to waste on such an ugly sight. "The ugly is a component of the beautiful," I said. You agreed. You were wrong, though you could not have known it at the time. The train station stands as proof of your error.

The sight of these half-human monsters huddling together beneath the vaulting archways of the station—if the founding architect only knew the ill use to which his wondrous creation would
one day be put—sickened me at first, then angered me, and then,
finally, struck me stone dumb. What can you say about a species
that is so susceptible to the blackening effects of a city, other than
that it is weak to the point of rot? It was left to Lily to remark
upon the place, once we had boarded the train and were safely on
our way. "Beastly," she said, letting the single word hang like the
man's maimed hand. After a short pause, I took up her thought.
"Oh, Lily," I said, "I am so happy to be traveling with you into the
country. It is in a rural setting that a man's soul—or a woman's,
for that matter—can truly flower. And so I will lavish my attentions on the petals of those flowers." Whether I said this in so
many words or said fewer and imagined the rest does not matter.
We were so close at that moment that speech and thought were one
and the same. You, too, have experienced this closeness with me,
wife, so you will be able to imagine. Lily and I were brought together by our idea of our union, which seems like either a paradox
or a tautology but is in fact both. I took Lily's hand, which was
so warm with desire that it seemed to heat the air around us, and
pressed it to my breast, and we listened to the click and the clack
of the train on the rails and at length fell into faultless sleep.

Time passed. The sun stretched out the shadows of trees,
which lay across the tracks like bridges. We crossed under one
of those bridges and then the train shuddered to a stop. We were
in the village where Mrs. Pritchard lived and where, more important, her house stood amid woods, meadows, and even a little
stream that wound through those woods and meadows. I had retained nearly every detail from Mrs. Pritchard's letter; that fine
old woman, though her shaky script betrayed her age, had an ap-

preciation of the power of description that rivaled my own. Lily went out ahead of me, carrying our luggage—we had managed to get most of our clothes in a single hard wheel case, although there were two other small bags that held my books and journals—and I followed. From behind I could read the sentence of her figure (particularly that which lay within parentheses). My mouth began to water. I felt a tremor in my thumb and index finger. Should I feel shame for that reaction? A man's hunger for a woman is part of nature, wife. In my time with you, I frequently saw the disclosed forms of other women. There is no point in apologizing for this. It was one of the imperfections of our union. I have forgiven you for your part in it, and I know that you will extend me the same courtesy. Since I have been with Lily, I have seen only one other woman in her natural state, and she was seventeen, and as such represented a false promise of fullness and flexibility. Her name was Mona, and she was my student in a course I had designed that sought to communicate the intimate link between poetry and nature. She was a good student, Mona, and she came by one afternoon to discuss the heartlessness of Tennyson's "In Memoriam." The topic undid us so completely that we had found ourselves, quite by accident, in my apartment, where I first checked to make sure that Lily was not present and then did my level best to direct the conversation toward those "orbs of light and shade" and those "wild and wandering cries" and away from the inevitable. I was not the teacher I hoped to be, though, because when I paused midway through what I thought was a rather convincing discourse, I saw Mona on the bed and her clothing in a heap on the ground beside it. Her hands were rounded in a kind of cage at the tops of her thighs. She opened the cage.

"These bags are heavy," Lily said, shattering my reverie.

"Are they?" I said.

"They are." She set them down. A less trained observer might have read the expression in her eyes as an appeal to me to relieve her of her burden, but I knew it for what it was—a reminder of what would occur later that afternoon, when we had snugged the bags in the corner of our new home. The suitcase that was now at Lily's feet contained all we would need for the afternoon's activities, including a hand mirror, a length of rope, and a razor that would prevent her from sinking into a barbarian state, especially about the legs and hips.

"It makes no difference to me," I said, answering her unasked question. "Dry or with a bit of shaving powder, entirely or in part. You decide."

She looked at me with feigned confusion—I learned that look from you, and also to dismiss it, and for that I am grateful—and we set off down the road leading to the cottage. Rustic life in all its glory was arrayed for us as if Mrs. Pritchard, or some other benevolent angel, had retained a troupe: there was an old woman waiting for the last of her pigs to ford a small stream and set off for home; there was a younger woman sitting beneath a tree and finishing with the needlework on a large tablecloth; there was a sunburned girl who was running from a sunburned boy toward a large tree that sat center-meadow, a god of the place.

While Lily went ahead with the suitcases, I stopped to inspect a leaf I saw at the side of the road. It reminded me, to be frank, of you: it was not a particularly spectacular specimen, and yet it was more spectacular than anything I could have imagined. The edge had browned slightly, and with it the vein skeleton. A corner had been eaten away by a beetle or one of the other divinely low creatures that flourished in this part of the country. It was a shabby thing that still communicated an indisputable beauty. "Lily," I called, but my voice was faint from wonder, and she did not hear me. I gripped that leaf by its petiole and took it with me, telling myself that this piece of evidence of the majesty of the everyday would be a great help when Lily and I reached our destination, dropped our bags, and settled into the narrow but sturdy bed that had been described to us in our correspondence with Mrs. Pritchard. I could place it on a table and watch it while the world turned upside down. Nature would steady us both.

I worried that Lily was so far up the path that she would reach the cottage before me, so I hurried to arrive before her. You know how fast I can run when I try. Still, this was done at great sacrifice to village life, or rather to my enjoyment of village life: to have any chance of arriving at the house before Lily, I had to rush through the characteristic scenes that were in abundance all around me, and as a result I have only the blurriest recollection of them. I do know that I saw a number of beautifully picturesque arrangements of flowers in neat little window boxes in front of neat little houses. I saw a woman spinning with a distaff in an enclosed porch. I saw a priest sitting sociably beside a young woman whose face was flushed a deep pink from what I can only assume was a sudden appreciation of the Lord's word.

My heart ached as I passed by these simple villagers, these simple tiles of benignity in the mosaic of the village, for I knew that it wanted little more than to settle among them and explore the common lines of fellowship and companionship. There would be time for that after the house, and Mrs. Pritchard's narrow but sturdy bed. Lily was ecstatic to be in the country. I had sensed it even before she herself had sensed it. Like you, she had spent most of her life in the city. Like you, she had been raised among its smokestacks and alleyways and fire escapes, and its adulterations were knit into her bones. On the train, Lily told me that one of her earliest memories involved playing hopscotch as a child, and confessed that as she grew older the numbers on the board came to represent a different sort of progress. I drew out from her a clearer sense of her meaning. She told me that she assigned a number to different levels of excitement. "Are you excited to-day?" I asked. She held up one hand, I assumed to give me a measure of her feelings. As was her habit, she did not offer a full account; she was generally embarrassed by the passions she felt. But her five fingers were stiffly raised. I verified her excitement by the traditional means, holding up three fewer, just before the conductor arrived to punch our ticket. When he departed, she drew me out as well, to the same end.

I will tell you a story that would embarrass a different sort of woman. The night before Lily and I left the city, I opened the window of my apartment and let her put her head out. Her hair was long and black and difficult to manage, in the fashion then popular in the city. I took my business with her then, just like that, with her head out of the window. "When we get to the country," I remember saying to her, "we will do this again, near a country window, and the air that you breathe will be new air. A little death, a little rebirth: Is this not what you want?" I cannot describe the expression she wore as she listened to me, mainly because I could not see her face, which was outside the window. The next day, on the train, her face was once again concealed from me. This time it was beneath a blanket I had draped over my lap. The conductor's curiosity did not recommend him.

At any rate, my dear wife, my memory of these clarifying moments caused me to walk faster along the path. I passed a stable that contained no horses but was rich with the promise of them, and then I passed a house in which I imagined country folk eating a hearty meal and exchanging simple tales of life and its triumphs and disappointments, and then I passed a lake upon which a swan drifted in silent judgment of any place less beautiful. Finally, I overtook Lily, who was huffing and puffing, trying to tug the suitcase through a section of the path that had gone soft from rain. My excitement was mounting, and I made sure she saw so as a form of incitement. She scowled at me to conceal her appetite.

I came to the house, fit the key in the lock, and pushed it open. There was a note on the table in the entryway welcoming us. The note was written on the inn's stationery, and there were more blank sheets beneath it, along with an envelope. I took the paper and envelope in my free hand and bounded up the stairs. The bedroom was just as Mrs. Pritchard had described it: small, Spartan, with a low table. I set the paper and envelope on the table and went to the window with the leaf I had taken from the path. A leaf contains a world, at least, and I held it there in my hand at the window, watching Lily struggle up the last stretch of path toward the house. She had given up carrying the suitcase and was now dragging it through beds of flowers, some that had recently bloomed and some that would never bloom. She could not see it from ground level, but there was beauty all around her. I twirled the stem of my leaf between my thumb and index finger. She did not see me, as she was not looking up. I let the leaf fall, like an invitation, and it landed in the soft grass just before the porch; as Lily tried to wrestle the suitcase up the stairs, her shoe came down directly upon it. I had given her the shoes—they resemble those I made you wear when we were fully man and wife. The heel pierced the leaf through the heart. It was a kind of murder. At that moment, I decided I would write you an account of the day. I would spare you not a single detail, from the morning train to the events of late afternoon that were about to unfold. I would tell you of Lily's hot breath, her wide eyes, the parts of her and the whole. I felt the prospect of it all thrum through me, and I undid my shirt and pants, and lay back on the bed, and waited for Lily to arrive.

A BUNCH OF BLIPS

THERE WERE A BUNCH OF BLIPS, ONE AFTER THE OTHER, BLIP, blip, blip. Rough and strenuous Richard was one; Donzac, deflated, another; the professor who called her "kitten," less ironically than she thought healthy; Jeff, the architect; Jack, the accounting intern; an outraged Iranian rich boy; a professional football player; a journalist; Louis from the Panhandle; Philip from Toowoomba. When Deborah had counted to ten, she stopped. Ten men had been inside her with varying degrees of success. She had held them, fondled, coaxed, teased, mocked, resented, occasionally admired. Now she was tired. Things weren't getting better. It was time for it to stop. She boarded a plane to Paris, where she resolved to continue her studies in form and composition. She would learn but not paint, and then return to Miami and paint what she had learned. A friend of a friend had an apartment that needed watching for the summer, a small place off the rue Beauregard, and she unlocked the door and pushed hard with her foot, as she had been told to do. "I am home," she said, trying not to make it sound like too much of a question.

Boatman, one of the few men who seemed to want nothing more from her than her friendship, was also in Paris, working in medical research. The first week she was there they met for coffee and he told her a story; it seemed incredible, yet he staked his word on it. A research department in a university had shown one thousand men a series of one hundred images. The images were broadly random: some were of trees, some of cars, some of animals, and some showed the faces of attractive women. At first, each image remained on screen for one second. Then the rate of projection was accelerated: each image was shown for only a half second, then a quarter second, then a tenth of a second. Finally the set of images was shown to the men in such rapid succession that each image was onscreen for only one twentieth of a second. At that point, the sequence was altered, the new sequence shown again at the fastest rate, and the men were asked which photograph was out of place. If they were unable to furnish an answer at that rate, the sequence was shown again at a slightly slower speed, and so on, until it was back to an image per second. The vast majority of the subjects showed no ability to answer correctly for the images of trees, cars, or animals, but nearly half the men were able to tell when images of women had been rearranged within the sequence, even at the fastest speeds.

Deborah had heard some fish stories in her day, and this ranked near the top.

"I'll bring you the magazine with the article," Boatman said. He pushed his cup of coffee forward as punctuation.

"You do that," she said, coming to her feet.

While she waited for the magazine, she poured herself into the books about painting she had brought from home. She spent time going slowly through museums. She talked on the phone to her mother more than she had in months. There were no men—there was no man—and that left her time. "We can have lunch every week," she told Boatman. "I'll even pay if you bring that magazine you lied about."

He presented it to her rolled up and rubber-banded. "Don't read it here at the table," he said. "It's rude. Wait until you get home." They ate. She went home. The magazine, thick and printed in an oversize format, was called *Topic: A Month of Things to Think About*. She was mortified that she had never heard of it and at the same time thrilled, because she was now permitted the pleasure of discovery, which was considerable. The magazine was a fantastic mix of high-toned reporting, lurid celebrity news, science, culture, home design, and travel. The cover story was about Corrado Feroci, an Italian sculptor who traveled to Thailand in the early twentieth century and created works at the behest of King Rama VI. Then came a piece about the metabolic studies of stressed cells, and then one about an actor who had left his wife for a costar. The print in some of the longer articles was tiny, but Deborah read every word, and when she looked up at the clock, more than an hour had passed. She went right back in for another hour, and called Boatman when she surfaced for dinner. "This is the best magazine in human history," she said. "I put it down, then picked it back up, and guess what story I landed on?"

"Metabolic studies of stressed cells?"

"No. A piece about Marcus Hebert."

"Who?"

"The French critic of accidental literature. Do you know him?"

"No," Boatman said. "The only French critic of accidental literature I know is no one." He waited a beat. "Jean-Marie No One."

"Hebert is a genius. He became famous writing these short essays about texts he would find in the street. Initially, he thought

they were the literary equivalents of ready-mades, but then he
designed this inverted critical structure that privileged a letter
you might write to a girlfriend over, say, Tolstoy."

"Well, of course," Boatman said. "Stupid Tolstoy."

"It got to the point where Hebert felt that the only way he
could make good on his theory was to stop publishing, and instead write his essays in the form of letters to other critics and
authors, who occasionally published them as correspondence. He
went on to write about the way that writing has changed: the
death of handwriting and the birth of typing, the death of words
as possessions and the birth of words as currency. Anyway, he
has a new book."

"A book? Hypocrite."

"That's addressed in this piece," she said. "Anyway, for years
he's been at American universities, but he's spending this whole
month in Paris. And because he's perverse to the end, he's doing
all kinds of things to alienate himself: staying in a different hotel
every week, staging a series of readings at rock clubs, speaking
only in English while he's here. I can't believe I didn't know that.
I can't believe this magazine."

"I told you."

"Though come to think of it, I can't find the article you mentioned, the one about the men studying images of women."

"What? Wait." She heard shuffling on the line. "Damn it. I
brought you the wrong issue. You have November and that article
is in December. I'll bring it the next time I see you."

"Or the time after that," she said. "No hurry." She had time.
Time had been returned to her. And now she had something to
fill it. When she hung up the phone with Boatman, she went immediately to the suitcase she had brought from Seattle, which was
now serving as a kind of bookcase. She pushed through until she

found the slim green volume of Hebert's work. She knew it by heart, almost, from the first sentence of the first essay ("It is lost to history who made one of the truer observations regarding our perceptual abilities") through the final sortie of those early years, "The Notepad and the Dictionary: Writing Down as a Form of Looking Up." She reread his work on the couch. She took the book to bed. She read in the bath. Hebert was with her everywhere, more than a lover was.

ON THE AFTERNOON OF HEBERT'S FIRST READING, weather threatened and then made good on its threat in the evening. By eight the streets were drenched, but there was no way she would be dissuaded. She had thought about asking Boatman to go with her—he was responsible, in a sense—but that ran counter to her ultimate goal.

Hebert looked as he looked on the promotional poster, which was a surprise. Usually such figures submitted outdated pictures of themselves out of vanity, but this one seemed accurate to within a few years. His hairline had receded early, and his skin was not so fine as a young man's. He held an unlit cigarette and waggled it around in a way that was comically French. He read a pair of short pieces, performed one longer one, and then read a new essay. "I have come back to my home country after a span of nearly a decade and found its character patently obvious from the first steps off the airplane," he said. "There is a poverty of minor detail and a surfeit of broad strokes, which makes it perfect for philosophy but in some way unsuited to artwork." Behind Deborah, a woman murmured and said, in nearly inaudible gospel, *"C'est vrai, dites-leur, c'est vrai."*

Afterward there was a reception. Hebert stood in the corner of the lobby where the walls were covered with a growing collection of posters for all the artists who had played at the club. He was directly beneath the poster for a band named Lowest Lane, whose lead singer was a woman who had filed her teeth to fangs. His cigarette was lit now. He seemed to need it. Deborah approached him.

"Will you sign this?"

"This is an old edition," he said. His tone was gentler than she had expected. "You don't see them very frequently."

"Well, I remember buying it in the bookstore in Seattle, during college."

"Ah," he said. "Seattle. A place I'll never be."

"You were there in spirit," she said, "through your book." She was laying it on thick, but that's what you were supposed to do. "You are in the city now?"

"I am."

She circled around. She showed leg when leg needed to be shown. She asked him where he was staying, and nodded approvingly. "Would you like to see it?" he said, and she did not answer right away, as if she was surprised, which allowed Hebert to feign a moment of embarrassment even as he was emboldened. Outside in the still-rainy night, the sky was many shades of gray. Hebert called a taxicab, one shade of yellow. At intervals he began to speak, and each time she cocked her head to show that she was listening. She took his hand in his hotel as they rode up in the elevator. The way to do it, she kept thinking, is just to do it. It reminded her of a sentence of his—"Opportunities will not represent themselves unless they are re-created and re-produced, and by that time they are less opportunities than products that carry the sense of opportunity"—and that made her laugh. She stifled her laugh by putting his hand in her mouth.

Hebert, though one of the sharpest and most original of modern thinkers, was uncomfortable in bed. His movements were sudden and seemed to have little to do with his pleasure. Deborah had always taken pride in her body, particularly in bed. It was one of the rare places where she could dominate and seem submissive. Here, though, she felt she was risking injury to Hebert. After working the bed from head to foot, they made their way to the couch. She sat there naked. He occupied the end closer to the window. "Do you believe that humans have bird songs?" he said. "By that I mean, do you think each of us has a native melody that, unsung or sung, represents us like a fingerprint?"

"Stop avoiding me," she said. Many thoughts drifted across his face, slowly at first and then quickened by the winds of his panic. He was triumphant, he was contrite, he was friendly, he was brusque. Mostly, he was limp, skinny, and pale, and she was delighted. Having gone at him, she could now set him aside. The power had shifted entirely. She had been wary of returning to men, but this was precisely why her decision was immoderate. She took a cigarette and stood by the window as he got dressed.

"Next week, I will be in a different hotel," he said. "And another after that."

"Well, then, I will see you in one of those," she said.

When she called Boatman the next day, she explained herself forcefully. "Got him," she said. "Two strikes, one after the other. The second time around he took it to me a little bit more. It was like he saw something on the surface and had the courage to go in after it."

"Right-o," Boatman said. He was as unfazed by her as ever. "Who's on tap for tonight? The prime minister?"

That night she read but retained little, and when she finally gave up, she did not sleep. She expected to have kept something from her time with Hebert: memories, pictures. But her recollection of the evening was pitch-black. She reread his book to try to jog her memory. The next night she painted better, but still no memories. She was drawing a deep blank. On Friday night, she went to a café down the street and allowed herself to be chatted up by a young French lawyer who loved to talk about automobiles and drugs and gourmet foods, after which she followed him to his apartment and engaged in a drunken and spirited session on a bed he had not bothered making from the night before. The morning after that, her memory of him was sharp, down to individual smells and textures. There was a patch of hair on his lower back. But she could recollect nothing of Hebert.

The following week, Hebert held another event at another rock club. She attended. He read. The audience was somewhat more hostile this time; a young man stood up without being acknowledged and challenged Hebert on his decision to speak only English. "Don't get so exercised about it, man," Hebert said, and enough of the crowd laughed that he was able to move on. Afterward there was a reception in the lobby, as before. Deborah stood in the corner with her legs crossed and watched Hebert work the room. It should have been a source of excitement to see him swerve from guest to guest. He noticed her and drew near. "Hello," he said. He was looking at her like she was already hooked, and she decided to play along. She heard a murmur ripple through the crowd standing near the door. In the cab he said nothing. In the elevator he said nothing. They sat on the edge of his bed and watched television. At last she grew impatient, reached into his pants without an invitation, and began to work on him. The result was not what she had expected. His entire body was consumed by a spasm of pleasure. He leapt up and plunged back down. "Oh! Oh!" he yelled. His face was as red as his eyes were bright. During the next hour he made love to her three times, each more intensely than the last. He took her out to sea. Stretched out beneath him, she wondered if she would forget this, too.

SHE DID, WITHIN A DAY. She shut her eyes tightly and tried to recover it, any part of it, but she could not. She did not even tell Boatman that she had gone back to Hebert. "I have a magazine for you," Boatman said. "How about lunch tomorrow?"

"I feel a little sick," she said.

She canceled a second lunch date and then the cures began to come in on two legs: Wilbon, who owned a watch shop; Denis, a musician; Leigh, a British actor who had worked briefly in adult films; Charles, an optometrist. She even considered a dalliance with Boatman, raised the issue with him at lunch. He looked at her, then burst out laughing, then took her hand in his. "I'm going to have to say no," he said. "I'd rather keep living through you, if that's okay." This she remembered down to the last precise thing—the streak of blue ink on Boatman's right hand, which had the appearance of a vein—but she could not retrieve a single detail about Hebert. She went back to read his essays, found them brilliant as always, but had no memory of the man. What did he smell like? How did he conduct himself while at her breast? "What is happening to me?" she asked Boatman. He laughed but said he didn't believe her. She flipped through the blips in her mind: the tall one, the skinny one, the goatee, the glasses. She could see them perfectly, but when she tried to come around to the other side of them, she could not. They were pictures in a deck of cards. She shuffled them, but it was no consolation. She called Boatman on the phone and was humiliated by the safety he felt.

She flew back to Miami on Labor Day weekend, leaving Hebert's book in the small apartment off the rue Beauregard. Still humiliated, she met a man named James at a party in a friend's backyard. He was large and dark and told her, soon after they met, that he thought of her as his girlfriend. "Oh?" she said. She was secretly pleased that someone was making this decision. On their fourth date he took her away for the weekend to a house he had bought with his ex-wife. "I always thought it needed a birdhouse," he said. He fashioned the birdhouse carefully, and it was a testament to his skills as a carpenter. He made a frame. He added a round front door and a window as decoration. He shingled the roof with tiny shingles and hammered in a perch just beneath the door. She watched him from the porch.

James stood back and looked at what he had made. Deborah called to him. Her voice turned him. Just then an untimely gust of wind arrived. It knocked down the umbrella post, which bumped against the table, which tilted downward. The birdhouse slid into the creek. "Well, hell," he said. "There it goes." And there it went. It floated down the creek until the creek fed the river and continued on down the river, turning as if with purpose whenever the river turned. People on the opposite bank saw the floating birdhouse and laughed at it, amazed. James came back inside the house, his face darkened by his failure. Deborah was sitting in a love seat rereading the magazine that Boatman had given her. The piece about Hebert quoted one of his famous statements, that music was a superior substitute for time itself: "What is not remembered in a song is kept nonetheless," he wrote, "because the next notes collect those that came before them." She looked at the picture that accompanied the article. That was exactly how he had looked when he had taken her to bed, or was it? James kicked the wall next to her chair. "I want that birdhouse to roast in hell," he said. She knew she would remember everything she was hearing. As she told Boatman on the phone that night, it wasn't so much what James said as the way he was saying it. "Hey," Boatman said. "That's exactly why I'm going to remember what you're saying now."

TO KILL THE PINK

I'M GOING TO MALAWI. I'M WRITING THAT DOWN ON A SINGLE sheet of paper, folding it into thirds, putting it into an envelope, and leaving it on the kitchen table leaning up against the sugar bowl. When I go, I don't want you to have any outstanding questions about where I've gone. Though most of your questions are outstanding. Pause. Get it? Remember when I used to do that, make a joke and then wait a minute before announcing it back to you like you were blind or deaf or dumb? I've been doing that to you ever since we were kids, ever since I nicknamed you Tails on account of your pigtails and it stuck. Fifteen years later you are a grown woman with a fine shape, top-shelf and bottom-drawer both, and it's that bottom drawer that lets the nickname live, even though I had to take off the *s*. I call you Tail sometimes because it makes you laugh and sometimes also makes you hot, but usually not in public, where you're Angie.

Last year I made a mistake in this regard, and I apologize. We were out for a walk, talking, and Lee Johnson who joined the seminary overheard our conversation and told me he thought the name was disrespectful to one of our beautiful sisters. I explained to him that it wasn't at all, that I was honoring one of the most divine aspects of you or any other sister, the woman's form, and that he could see how it was intended if he watched me when I bent down in the morning to kiss you good-bye before I went off to the radio station for my shift. You are a beautiful sleeper. You are beautiful awake, too, except when you try to be funny, which is why you shouldn't try to be. You look good, like I said. You're morally certain. You notice things about people and comment upon them in a manner that almost always leads to improvement. You're full of more love than hate. Why bother with funny? Leave that to me. You can come visit me in Malawi.

Let's go back twelve days. You go first, and when you get there, take everything off and slip into bed. When I arrive, I'm bound to be disoriented and dispirited from the trip—no one likes going backward—and I want to get a little sugar before I head out into the cruel summer. You can leave the black bra on if you want. It does its job in the way of shaping and holding but is camouflaged against what you always like to call your African complexion. The first time you told me that, you were fourteen, maybe, and I was a year older, like always, and I was running with your brother Larry in that gang he had for a little while before he decided to become an accountant. Tough guy. The gang was called the Tigers, and Larry said we had to snatch a purse for initiation. I didn't want to, so I went around to all the girls I knew and asked them if they had a spare purse I could borrow. The first two girls I asked looked at me crooked, like maybe I was going to wear it for my own pleasure, but you just said "sure" and ran upstairs and got me one. It was black and you said you preferred bright colors to go with your African complexion. "Complexion?" I said. "But Africa's so simple. See lion, flee lion." I paused. "Get it?" I said. "No cars, no bars, no drugs, no hustlers. Just a lion wanting you to be his lunch."

You set your mouth in a straight line and sat down on the steps. "Rennie," you said. "I won't have you mocking Africa. It's where we all come from. The Harlem that you see around you wouldn't exist if we hadn't been loaded into boats against our will. You're a light-skinned man, but you can't pass for white, so don't go thinking you can turn an eye on the place you came from." It was the first time I noticed that you got more beautiful when you got mad.

"Actually," I said, "I know for a fact that my ancestor wanted to come. He tied himself up and hopped into the boat. He got a little sick of baobab stew and thought he might prefer some soul music and American movies."

I thought you'd scoff at me, or at best laugh the way girls always laughed, their eyes bright but their body leaning back. Instead, you leaned forward so I could better see the twinkle in your eyes "Not funny," you said. "That's a historical tragedy and you're getting A-list material from it. If you call that A-list. Please don't make these jokes around me anymore."

I put a hangdog expression on, though my heart was leaping. "I'll make a note of that," I said, "and put it in my purse."

Here I was sure you'd finally lean back, but you jumped off the steps and threw your arms around my neck. "You heard me," you said. "No more jokes." Then you kissed me on the side of the face, but it was like you were kissing my lips. A girl went by behind you on roller skates. A leaf fell off a tree. There were so many other details that I'll never recover, little things I wish I could have noticed. Instead, I was in the grasp of something broader, thicker, and darker. So were you: that is a joke but it is after the fact.

That took us back more than twelve days. Sorry. You try keeping your mind from the memory of our first kiss. Let me reset the time machine. Twelve days ago, on Saturday, we were having coffee and toast in my apartment, where you had been living since late spring. "Like a real couple," I said. This was my move: to state the thing that truly amazed me, with a bend in my tone to make it seem like I was taking it all in stride. In my mind, I called it the Twistback. I was reading the newspaper; you were looking out the window. That's how breakfasts went. I always brought a book or a paper. You liked to start the day making sense of the world with your eyes. Between us, we had it all covered. Near the bottom of the front page, there was an article about Malawi, newly independent from Britain. "Isn't that strange?" I said. "That a country can be newborn after it's been around a while?"

You tracked a bird across the window, left to right, before you answered. "It didn't used to be called Malawi," you said. "What was it again? Hyasaland? Something like that?"

"Nyasaland," I said. "If it was high-ass-a-land, they would have elected you president." I paused. "On account of the ass you have on you," I said.

You ignored me, which was a form of accepting the compliment. "I'm all for independence," you said. "The only problem is that sometimes when these states go that way, they end up like children who need a parent, and the parent is some dictator-for-life who never treats the people like they're people." You crunched your toast between your teeth.

"How a twenty-four-year-old black girl who's never been out of New York City knows so much about the world never ceases to amaze me," I said. Again, the Twistback.

"Well, I always paid attention to where I came from," you

said. "While you were busy studying the human comedy, I was trying to figure out human drama."

"You're the sad mask; I'm the happy mask," I said. "Takes both of us to put on a play."

"I don't have time to put on a play," you said. You were studying to be a lawyer, and the fact that you seemed unencumbered in the morning was only the shadow of the way you were at night: walled in by textbooks and mimeographed papers, ballpoint pen in your mouth, glasses pushed high on your head. Many times I'd go to bed by myself, and you'd show up hours later, slipping silently between the sheets. I wasn't asleep, but I didn't let on, and you didn't go to sleep either, but rather stayed up repeating names to yourself: names of cases, names of judges, names of laws. That exercise filled your mind with answers, but overnight the answers turned into more questions, which you liked to ask me in the morning. That morning the questions were about belief, or at least they started that way. You asked me if I could believe that there was a time in our country's history when there were no penalties for obstructing minority access to a polling place.

"Black people can vote?" I said, "Heavens to Betsy. No one told me."

"I just get tired of this sometimes," you said.

I felt a chill race down my spine. "This?" I said, waving my arm around the kitchen like a TV pitchman. "But it has everything."

"Not this," you said. "This, America, now. We're all working to make it better, except for the ones who are working to make it worse. But it all goes so slow." You looked out the window for the bird, another form of progress. You crunched your toast again. "Have you ever thought of visiting Africa?" you said.

"Why?" I said. "I like wearing pants. That way, I can take them off when I want to get with you."

"Be straight for a minute," you said. "It's where you came from, the place that created both your problems and your promise. Aren't you curious? You really should go."

"You go."

"I'm broke as a joke."

"I have money, but do you really want me to crack open my Diamond Ring Fund?"

Usually this got you to stop: it was marriage talk, which sent you off into a speech about how you didn't believe in marriage, that it was only a ceremony to verify a love that, if truly felt, didn't need a ceremony for verification, that you were wary of entering an arrangement that made you formally dependent upon another human being, let alone an abstract idea that shared more with slavery than with salvation. This was the only time you seemed as though you were joking, and it was when you were at your most serious. You had been doing it as long as I had known you; Larry used to say you were a secular preacher with the whole world as your congregation. "I'm just saying that even a pea-brained rising radio star might want to reconnect with his own identity now and again."

"Not guilty as charged," I said. It's true that I worked at a radio station, that I played a little music, made a few jokes on the air, pocketed a bit of dough. It advanced my reputation to some small degree, or, I like to say, at least cemented my reputation as a man who can only be advanced by small degrees. But I was secretly proud of what I did. I leavened moments in people's days that were otherwise leaden. I offered a balm for the spirit. I encouraged people toward the divine without resorting to anything godly. "But if I see a pea-brain, I'll let him know," I said. I got up to put my plate in the sink, and I took yours, too, and you said, "Thank you," and whatever little bit of tension was rising in the room dissipated. We went to the couch and listened to records and you let me kiss your neck a little bit. "I'm just saying," I said, "I'm happy here in America. I know there are problems. There's always going to be problems. I know we were kept down, and we're rising up too slowly. But I also know other things. Do you hear what we're hearing? Is there another place you can listen to Marvin Gaye and then the Beatles and then Chuck Berry and then Mary Wells and feel like you really know what they all mean? I love being here in this place and I love being here in this place with you."

"It is nice," you said, nuzzling into my shoulder.

"I would recognize this country even from the back," I said. "You think I need to investigate my identity? This is my identity." Then I headed off to work and proved my point, played "Stubborn Kind of Fellow" and "I Want to Hold Your Hand" and "Thirty Days" and "Your Old Standby," all as messages to you.

That was twelve days ago. I didn't even fold up the paper with the news about Malawi. I left it open on the couch, and that night, when I got home from work, I rolled you into it when we were getting down to business. Then a week passed, and it was five days ago, and it was so hot that we went out for ice cream and ended up talking to some of the kids we knew in the neighborhood. Ken Louis was there, who told everyone he was related to Joe Louis, and his best friend Paul Ordis, who liked to tease Ken by saying he was related to Joe Ordis, and James Powell, who was the worst of the bunch but still a good kid. They all had girls they were sweet on, and they wanted you to give them advice on how to act. "Don't act like this one," you said, pointing at me, and all three of them bagged up. Paul Ordis said he hoped one day he'd have a girl as pretty as you, and he meant it so sweetly that you told him you were sure one day he would. Then I told him stories about me and Larry and how we both got it together in time for adulthood. "You can call him Larry, CPA," I said. On our way back we saw two white cops sitting in a car at the corner. One made a gun with his finger and pointed it out the window. He was laughing.

That night we were closer in bed, though we couldn't have been any closer, and not for any major reasons. It was as a result of a host of little reasons: seeing the teenagers on the stoop near the ice cream shop and remembering when we were that age, knowing how pretty you were and how smart you were and how clearly you saw the world and wondering if I could do the right things to keep you. There was a slight metallic uneasiness in my head, and I assume there was in yours, too, and that's why you let me make love to you the way I did. "You know what I mean," I said afterward. "Competently." You threw your arms around me and laughed.

We both knew enough to be uneasy about the kids and the cops, but we never thought the two stories would come together the way they did. The following week it was even hotter, and all the kids in the neighborhood were out in the street, acting foolish. A group of about five of them, including Paul Ordis and James Powell, were play-fighting, mostly to make fun of Ken Louis, though they continued even after he left to go home. The play fight got louder and louder, and finally one of the neighbors called the cops, just as another neighbor came out of his door to stop the boys. James Powell was in bold character now, and he stood up tall to the man who came to stop the fight. "What do you want?" he said. "What the hell do you want, man?" The neighbor sprayed James and Paul with a hose, and James pretended to go wild and ran full-speed after him, shouting that he was going to kill him when he got hold of him. That was when one of the cops who had showed up on the scene emptied his service revolver into James's back. I wasn't there, and neither were you, but you were one of the first people Paul Ordis saw when he ran crying home. "Miss Angie," he said. He couldn't say any more and he buried his face in your shoulder.

I was at work, spinning records and making jokes, when the calls started to come in about the shooting. I did what I swore I would never do, and that was to feel ashamed that my job wasn't serious enough for the world around it. I took the records off the turntable and let people know what was happening, how the CORE meeting later that day was now going to be a protest, how demonstrations were being planned for the next day and the day after that in Harlem and Brooklyn. Already the violence was starting, a few kernels of corn popping. I didn't come home until late, and when I did, you greeted me at the door like a wife, silently embracing me and whispering into my ear that you were proud of me. "How can you be proud of anyone today?" I said. That night you didn't stay up late studying. You went to bed when I did, and we were distant from one another, each in our own head, though we couldn't have been any closer.

We ate breakfast silently the next morning. The newspaper was unopened on the table next to me. You were looking at the window as if no one would ever be able to see through it again.

"Angie," I said.

"Why not Tail?" you said. "You should call me what you want, and I know you want it." It was a burlesque only. I could no more have touched you that way than I could have killed you. I kissed you chastely and went off to work, hoping for the best. I didn't get the best. I didn't get anywhere near the best. The demonstrations started peaceful but didn't stay that way for long, and before you knew it there were cars burning and bricks crashing into windows. What would Lee Johnson have said about any of it? I was at work again, imagining I had a new job, which involved keeping the people calm. I was at work again, failing. The calls were pouring in about how the neighborhood had already slipped out of civilization and the city was soon to follow. In the afternoon I took a call from an older white man. "I've been listening to your show, and I have a solution," he said.

"Sir?" I said.

"You should go back to Africa."

I had heard it before, of course. We all had, and much worse. But this time it sounded different. The man wasn't angry. He had the appearance, at least on the phone, of a rational being. "Sir?" I said again.

"You heard me," he said. "Go back. We don't need you here."

His comment went through my head, brick-through-window-style, and with it went many other things: affronts, confusions, challenges I had to his remark, ways I could respond. I reversed the process, pulled the brick out until the window was intact again, and in the reflection I saw a clear picture in which I had the man down on the ground, my hands around his throat. I was squeezing hard, yet it was eliciting only laughter, flushing his face a healthy pink from his cheeks to the roots of his hair. I tried to kill the pink and instead I intensified it; his face went red, then purple, then darkened until it was like mine, then darkened further until it was like yours. I put the phone to my ear and heard only the dial tone.

I left work, crisscrossed streets where I shouldn't have felt safe but did. A store that sold fish tanks was burning. Pause. Get it? I directed myself to believe that fire was a refining force, just

as I had once believed that humans are capable of kindness, or
that jokes offer an adequate defense against cruelty. You weren't
at the apartment. I went to the library, then I went to a liquor
store—both intoxicants, neither lasting—and then I went home
and called a travel agent and asked how much it would cost to fly
from Kennedy Airport to Blantyre.

"Blantyre?" the girl on the line said. She wasn't being rude,
just curious.

"The one in Malawi," I said, "not in Scotland. Though I can
see how my accent may have confused you." It was possibly the
last joke I had in me, and not one I was particularly proud of.

"Yes, sir," said the girl, flustered, and got right on it.

When she told me the arrangements were made, I asked her if
I really wanted to do this.

"Sir?" she said.

"Nothing," I said. "Nothing at all." I looked through the book
I had taken from the library. The city of Blantyre, named for the
birthplace of the explorer Livingstone, was in the highlands,
which may have strengthened the resemblance. It was surrounded
by four mountains whose names I committed to memory—Soche,
Ndirande, Chiradzulu, Michiru—and which I imagined as a vocal
quartet performing on a street corner: first tenor, second tenor,
baritone, bass. There was a joke there, but I didn't reach for it.
The book had some pictures, including one of a woman standing
out in front of a small bank, facing away from the camera. She
looked just like you. I shut the book and put it away so that you
wouldn't see it, and then I did what I had been waiting days to do:
I took a nap. I dreamed of you when you were a little girl. You had
your pigtails on and you were telling other girls jokes that were
labored and earnest. You were trying to be better. You always
were. Ten years from now I want to be holding you in my arms

and kissing you while we listen to our children playing in the next room, and to do that I have to be newly born so that I am no longer so young. Isn't it strange that a man can be newborn after he's been around a while? I hope you don't misunderstand what I'm doing with this trip. On the plane I will say prayers because I don't like flying and also because I am trying to find the divinity in many things. On the plane I will cry because I have doubts, and then I will take the *s* off and have doubt. On the ground I will stay in my hotel the whole time except for quiet walks on the street. On the ground I will spend the nights reading until I understand and spend the mornings looking out the window. Let's move forward twelve days, to when I will come back to you with my heart recharged and my vision restored. "I will reconnect," I wrote in the note I will leave for you, and I imagine that when you read that you'll lean forward, eyes bright. Even if you don't understand the way I made the decision, understand that I want to be able to be the way I need to be for you, to make you laugh and make you want to laugh some more, and I just don't see that happening if I stay around here too much longer.

WHAT WE BELIEVE
BUT CANNOT PRAISE

THEY TELL YOU TO PLAN FOR CHANGE, BUT WHAT THEY REALLY mean is to plan for time, whether it changes things or not. As a result of family business, I was recently called back to the town where I grew up, a flat and sunbaked stretch of suburban south Florida. In the years since I left town, much of it has been torn down or overbuilt. For most of the two days I spent there, I felt more dislocation than location: the squat white shack where I traded in the faulty rental car had once been a veterinary practice, the firm handling my uncle's probate was housed in a glass-and-steel tower that rose up from what was once a strip mall anchored by an optometrist and a sandwich shop. The third day in town, already bored by what was new, I undertook a tour of deliberate nostalgia. I drove past my high school, past the park where I had played Little League, past creeks I fished and trees I climbed and even the house of the first girl I had ever loved, whose last name I didn't remember and whom I had been too afraid to approach until junior high school, when it was too late. I parked across the street from the house and wondered who lived there now. I backed out, drove away, made one left turn and then another. I was looking for the real estate office where my mother had worked one summer, only to quit in tears after a fight with the office manager; instead I came upon a small tan building that I recognized for what it no longer was: the law firm where I had worked one summer during college. It had occupied only a small corner of my life, that job, but it was dense with implication. The building looked exactly as it had then, but because time had passed and, by passing, shifted nearly everything within me, the sameness of the place was more shocking than any change I could have imagined. I got out of the car and scrutinized the nameplates to the left of the main glass doors; the names were unfamiliar enough to comfort me, but I was still not entirely comforted. As I pulled away, I glanced in my rearview mirror and imagined that I saw myself there, standing by the glass doors. It was a highly theatrical arrangement, and it drew me in, by degrees, until the present was far behind me and the past was present.

Schiff and Mortenson, the two principals at the firm, had trained together, and each was convinced of the other's skill. In fact, the name of the practice was itself a testament both to that conviction and those skills. Schiff, the younger of the two, had suggested that Mortenson's name should come first, in keeping with alphabetical order and the superior experience of the older man. Mortenson parried Schiff's proposal by arguing on behalf of euphony and meter, the way the name would be spoken by men when they spoke it. He was giving up his dominance, but he was justifying his decision with reasons of wisdom, and in this he further demonstrated his preeminence. For the most part, this was the way the talents were assigned: protocol to one man, strategy to the other. They knew that they were held in balance by one another, and that this balance was what kept them from tipping toward either collision or drift.

Schiff's parents were German immigrants, and he had kept on in that same spirit. He had skin that was pink like a baby's and arms that at first seemed short but were in fact only thick. The features of his face were mostly absent, pushed down into the pudding of his flesh. He had the appearance of something not just fat but fattened. His girth made dressing an ordeal for him, which was probably why he insisted on automating the process: each day, he wore a light-blue shirt beneath a dark-blue coat, and brown pants above black shoes. The only bit of improvisation he permitted himself was his tie: one day a solid yellow, one day green, one day red, all rendered in the fullest and most deeply satisfying shades. He was older than his years, older than all of ours. "We have tagged a specimen of *Tristissimus hominum*," Mortenson liked to say of his partner, with comically formal pronunciation.

Mortenson was another kind of species: easier to tag, harder to be made to understand that he had been tagged. He was not as fat as Schiff; he was not fat at all, except if you watched him for a while and began to understand that he thought that he deserved everything around him. All his features were on the sharp side of strong, from nose to ears to chin. There was only one part of his anatomy that had no point: his head was a perfect bald dome, as round as if it had been scooped out from something. He was a decade Schiff's senior but quicker, healthier in body and mind alike, the kind of eternally young middle-aged man who would sometimes leave the office in the afternoon to swim laps for an hour in his health club's pool. He had held on to youth with the same effortful ease that characterized nearly everything he did. His enthusiasms—for cars, for women, for the law, though not all of it—were too present in him, and Schiff was always bringing him back to the moment by placing a heavy finger upon some line or other of testimony or statute. "I can't be bored for you," Mortenson would say to Schiff, his eyes twinkling, but he could be, and was, excitedly. He had given himself fully to the law as practice, to the artifice of it that men like Schiff insisted was merely a protective cover for a dense moral core, and he held an ever deeper belief that the core, far from pure, might itself be broken open and inspected for even more precious traces of artifice.

At home, as at work, Mortenson was Schiff's counter. He was married, to a second wife only slightly more than half his age, but he was not very serious about the matter. He liked to take the secretaries out for lunch and to treat them to drinks after work. The secretaries never lasted very long in his employ, though I noticed that they didn't seem to leave angry. It was another one of his many talents. When secretaries left, I would sometimes get a call in the evening and orders to open the office in the morning. That's the door I was looking at in my rearview mirror as I drove away from the office. The door was closed, but it had opened a memory. When I got to the edge of the parking lot, I thought I was far enough away that it was safe to relax, because I was safe from that memory. I was wrong on only one point, which is enough.

I ARRIVED AT WORK one rainy June morning, fresh from my first year of college, bearing a note of introduction from my father, who had attended college with Mortenson and was now a professor of political history at the local university. He was a principled man, my father, though his first principle was to seek validation.

"Gregory Tipton, junior," Mortenson said, though I went by Jim and always had. He read my father's note, which I had not

been permitted to see, with a hard light in his eyes that soft-
ened to something more hospitable by the time he reached its end.
Then he came to his feet, motioned for me to follow, and took me
to the file room. "Get acquainted with the place," he said, and left
me there.

I got acquainted with it at once, and then spent the rest of that
long summer wishing I had not done so with such swiftness. The
room had no windows. It was lit by massive fluorescents. Three
of its walls were lined from ceiling to floor with beige filing draw-
ers, while the fourth contained, in addition to the door, a map
that showed the countries of those continental cabinets: which
of them were inhabited by past judgments, which by pending
arguments, which civil litigation and which criminal. There was
exactly one piece of art in the room, a picture of two fish jumping
from a stream side by side, tails fully fanned.

After my first morning there, I emerged to find Mortenson
smiling and chatting with a secretary. "Go get yourself some
lunch and then alphabetize and file the pile by the door," he told
me. That took care of the afternoon and the next day. The hours
piled up and I filed them away, too. On the morning of the third
day, a knock sounded at the door and Schiff appeared. He stood
in the doorway until I invited him in, then took a seat dolor-
ously and asked me how I was enjoying the file room. When I
murmured something about getting an education, he cleared his
throat to take me off it. "The files are history, but what's history? Merely markers of time that can't be recovered." This was, I
would come to learn, his dominant mode, a grave melancholy that
he intended as philosophy but was in fact autobiography. "Well,
this is what Mortenson wants you to do, so you should work," he
said, "and I should go."

But he did not go; he stayed with one hand hovering just

above the folders and began to instruct me, slowly but with un-
mistakable purpose, in the law. That first day's lesson was the
Jeffers case, which concerned a client who had sued his employer
for unlawful dismissal. Schiff was not capable of fine movements,
but his broad strokes had all the necessary detail in them: he
explained the man's position, the employer's stance, the statute
at that time, the dominant interpretation of that statute, the prec-
edent that allowed him to locate an opening. Through it all, it was
clear that the law had once meant everything to him, and now
meant nothing. He was bereft but not poor; only a rich man could
have lost so much. Finally, after we had toured the whole of the
case, he stirred heavily. "After lunch, come by my office. I have
some work for you that makes more sense than this. I'll leave it on
the table by the window."

His office was in the corner. As in the matter of the firm's
name, Mortenson had asserted his stature by concession, giving
up the largest space on the floor to his partner. Schiff kept the
place sparse. He had no pictures with which to clutter the desk
or credenza, and no newspapers or magazines. The place was
not empty but filled with what was missing. The assignment for
me—a list of appointments I was supposed to schedule—was on
the table, squared between two staplers.

When I finished, it was late. Nearly everyone had left for the
day. From Schiff's window I could see the spire of the university
lecture hall where my father held forth on Lewis Douglas and the
Bonus Bill. There was, just beneath the window, a small triangu-
lar park, trees springing up from each corner, a small pond in the
dead center—no more than a pool, really, for bicycles and baby
carriages to circle—and spans of grass in which children tossed a
ball. The afternoon light played out, and by degrees my reflection
appeared on the window glass. It was unfamiliar to me, and in the

midst of so much newness that unfamiliarity was a haven. I had a clear sense of becoming something I had not been before.

Schiff visited me in the file room only once that week, and once the week after that. Each time he lectured in that understated, overdetermined manner of his, and each time he departed with some word or another about work he had for me in his office. As we went, I came to forget the specifics of the cases he presented and to remember only the aphorisms with which he summed up each case. At the conclusion of a long case concerning workplace injury, he represented the judgment to me with this moral: life is a bell with a crack in it, and yet its tone when struck is the nearest to perfection any man will ever know.

It is hard for me to explain exactly what I did in the file room the first part of that summer. The firm had started as a civil-rights concern but under pressure from Mortenson had shifted its business toward anticorporate litigation: a pharmaceutical company that had not adequately advertised the health harms of its products, a shipbuilder that had exposed its workers to irresponsible levels of asbestos. I summarized existing documents, copied new blanks, arranged and assembled. I did not work with any great speed, because I enjoyed staying late, past Schiff and Mortenson, past the secretaries. I liked the office when it went quiet and cool with evening light. It was as if I were the last man on Earth, and I insisted on that belief even when I heard the cleaning lady's cart clattering its way down the hall. I felt lonely, and in full possession of my loneliness. It was the first time I had owned anything of value.

ON FRIDAYS, Schiff and Mortenson rounded up the secretaries and the paralegals and the office manager, ordered food, and sat in the conference room. The two of them did not agree on many things, but there was no argument here: Chinese. The restaurant was run by a man who had not a drop of Chinese blood in him, but that's how it was done in those days. We put it out, the moo goo gai pan and chicken chow mein and barbecued spare ribs, and we flipped our ties back over our shoulders and tucked napkins into our collars and got to it.

"Pass that carton, please," Mortenson said.

"Here you go," Schiff said. He was eating. He was a man who ate. But while the rest of us sat around the table and talked about our week, he held himself back from the discussion. His gaze went to the window, though he had a way of giving you to understand that he was looking at the pane of glass rather than through it.

"It's a nice day out there," said one of the paralegals, a young woman with a brunette bun.

"That it is," Mortenson said. "Don't you think?" he asked Schiff. Schiff didn't answer, and this spurred Mortenson on. "I saw a movie the other day," he said, pointing his chopsticks— and the shrimp pinched between them—at his partner. "Exciting. About a man who tries to kill the president of an African nation. It's based on fact." He knew which part of the sentence shone most brightly to his partner, because he repeated it. "Can you imagine?" he said. "An assassin."

"I don't like it when they make a movie about something like that," Schiff said, bringing his large head around. "The very point of an assassin is that he is trying to be as famous as the man he assassinates. The film shouldn't conspire with a murderer to that end."

"What do they call the man they're trying to assassinate? The assassinee?"

"He is the assassination. That's the noun for the victim as well as the process."

"I didn't know that," said Mortenson.

"It's a fact," said Schiff, "though not a pretty one. What we believe but cannot praise."

Mortenson was unwilling to be drawn into the other man's current. "Well," he said, "this movie has a great sequence where the assassin is assembling his weapon to practice for the fateful moment," said Mortenson. "He is in a bedroom at the home of his girlfriend, and there is a baby sleeping in the corner. It's a melo-dramatic contrast, but somehow it's very affecting."

"Well, I don't like the whole business of it," Schiff said. "It's distasteful."

"Also, in the film, many of the Africans are wearing American T-shirts. And not just any shirts. Did you know that after sports championships are played, the shirts announcing the victory of the losing team, which have of course already been printed, are shipped to Africa? It's like there's an alternative reality there."

"Or here," Schiff said. And that is how it went. Mortenson moved from subject to subject, like a child discovering the very process of discovery, and Schiff functioned punctuationally, al-ways with a heavy sense of judgment. It was like watching two painters work side by side; Mortenson with more colors in his palette, Sciff furnishing the sense of form.

Toward the end of the meal, they turned to practical matters, specifically to personnel, and to the sense that they would have to settle a few questions before they went away again. They were traveling often that summer, as they were handling a pair of cases involving police shootings of unarmed young men in central Flor-ida and southern Georgia. After they had returned from the previous trip, one of the secretaries had left—the rumor, as usual, was that it had to do with Mortenson—and Amy, one of the other secretaries, was out on maternity leave. "We're down two," Schiff said, "and we need someone new." They discussed the issue in front of everyone, which was their way.

"What's your feeling about Lisa Foster?" Mortenson said.

"Who?"

"The Foster girl. I told you the other week. We got a letter of application. She wants a summer position. Or we could promote Jim here to a real job." He swiveled the chopstick toward me.

"Promotions take time," Schiff said, sighing with a heaviness that would have, in another man, been comic. "Lisa is her name? Her father's the doctor?"

"A hell of a doctor."

"Let's have her in for an interview."

"I jumped the gun on this one," Mortenson said. "I had Stacy schedule her for tomorrow morning."

"I'll be here," Schiff said.

No one asked me, though I would, as it turns out, be most affected by the whole business.

WHEN LISA FOSTER FIRST CAME into the office, it was out of the rain. She shook off a coat and then lifted the damp hair away from her face. It was light to the point of white, even when wet. I knew her from around town: her father was a doctor who had treated my mother for something mysterious years before, and who had come by the house with a dignified look on his face while she was dying. He was an unhealthy man himself who somehow managed to look like a matinee idol. His wife was a compact blonde whose features were harder than she would have wished. And yet they combined perfectly in their daughter, who was short and buxom, a bit flat in the nose and deep in the eyes, and so powerfully attractive that when she entered the office I stepped out from behind the filing cabinet and took her coat without thinking.

"Thank you," she said, and the way she neglected to say my name told me that she knew it. Mortenson appeared and took her into the conference room, where Schiff was waiting. I sat and covered the front desk for Stacy, who was late. Or rather: I pretended to cover for Stacy and I watched Lisa Foster. Her face did not look like the face of a stranger. Everything about her reminded me of another woman, but when I thought of those other women I was reminded of her. Inside the room, Mortenson asked questions with false seriousness, and Schiff occasionally gave an equally false laugh.

She got the job, of course. I don't think it was ever in question. Her father, it seemed, had also treated Mortenson's wife on a matter some years before. "Just in time," Mortenson said, though he did not elaborate. They put her behind a boxy desk up front that was fenced in by a putty-colored partition. She said hello every day to everyone as they came through the door. To me, she gave a little wave that at first seemed like no more than professional obligation. When I decided, quite independent of any evidence, that she was not the kind of woman to act out of obligation, I started waving back.

LISA WAS A TALENTED GIRL—she was a fine painter who was also taking classes in architecture—but perhaps her most important trait was her lack of belief in herself, which in turn produced a fine brand of aggression. When I made a comment, she would contest it, no matter what it was. If a joke failed to find its mark, as it often did, she would tell me flatly why it was unfunny. "I'm assertive, not aggressive," she told me. "One is about protecting your own space; the other is about moving into someone else's." I accepted the definitions but not the diagnosis. That first week, she stopped me as I went downstairs for lunch. "I'll join you," she said. "Let's eat in the little park."

We went across the street to a bench, which was in a shady, quiet spot that seemed all the more so after the hot, crowded stretch of road we had to cross to get there. We put our sandwiches out on the table and weighed down napkins with bottles of juice. Afterward, she smoked a cigarette. That first day, we didn't have what I would call a full conversation. She made observations about the people in the office and I agreed, usually readily. She knew Mortenson was a wolf even before Stacy confessed to her in the women's bathroom. "He takes her to motels," she said, "not because he can't go to her place, but because he kind of gets off on the sleaziness of it. He's a good judge of character, though. She said she does, too." Schiff, she held, was a great man. "But the kind of great man no one will ever know. He's so shy. He turns away from me when I'm talking to him. And to have a man that large turn away? It's a blow to the ego." She told me that her life as an artist was, while not temporary, not necessarily permanent. "Not that I'll ever stop painting, but I have a feeling that later on I might want money, or things that I can get with money. I don't know how I'll handle being poor down the line." She said she enjoyed working in the office, that she imagined that she was ordering the world, or at least giving order to a part of it in a way that might spread outward, like a healthy disease.

The next day at lunch, I was a little bolder, sometimes frowning at things she said, sometimes laughing. The third day, I spoke up. "I remember coming to this park as a kid," I said. "Fourth of July."

"Really?" she said. "Me too. I was afraid the fireworks would fall on me, and I hid under that tree over there."

"Oh, I remember you now," I said. "The coward." Insulting her, even in jest, was not an easy thing, but it yielded the desired result. She laughed and moved closer to me on the bench; between us there was a thin band of heat. She had also fallen silent, which was rare, and I had time to study her: the way her clothes, which were always tight, seemed insensible to her dimensions. That night, when I thought back on the day, I felt a thickness in the pit of my stomach. I had a girlfriend back at college, almost, and another girl who was waiting if that didn't happen. Lisa could have been a summer fling, but she was not a summer fling. Her center of gravity was too low. It was wrong of me to hope for her, because my life was loaded up, and she was not the thing that would, if added, make it lighter.

Still, if I was content not to have her, I also did not want to watch her go elsewhere, and I made a point of keeping our lunch plans at least twice a week. For her part, she clearly felt some displeasure at her own excitement as well, and so she leveled the frame by reminding me of her power at every opportunity. She started to mention a recent ex-boyfriend named Alan and a number of unnamed suitors. There were also accompanying gestures, like reaching up to arrange her hair and, in the process, showing me the undersides of her bare arms before bringing down those arms and folding them across her chest. The whole effect was masterful; she aroused excitement while at the same time foreclosing any possibility of acting on that excitement. Because it was what I wanted, too, it drew us closer together.

"So," Lisa said at the beginning of the third week, at the end of lunch, as she lit her cigarette. "Good weekend?"

"Not much to speak of," I said.

"Well, then don't," she said, laughing. "I'll tell you about mine instead. I had a friend in town from college, and we went to a party on Saturday night."

"A good party?"

"A long party. A leave-at-four-in-the-morning-not-quite-remembering-your-own-name party. We smoked a ton of who knows what. But I wouldn't say it was good. At the moment, I'm more into peace and quiet. Trying to focus on work."

"Office work or painting work?"

She tapped out the cigarette. "That's an interesting question, although you might not know it."

I scowled at her. "Thanks, I guess."

"I mean it. People think that because I paint, painting has to come first. But painting is observing, so it always comes second. What comes first is observing: a party, or my family, or this office. Yesterday I was watching how Schiff stands when he's waiting for the elevator. He bows his head and turns one leg inward, like he's trying to disappear. How can a big man disappear, really? He's disrespecting physics. But it's like he thinks that the elevator ride might be his last, and he's not sure that he minds the idea."

"You got all that from watching him for a few minutes?"

"It's been a few weeks," she said. "But I'm getting sick of sitting in the beige cage. I want to be able to move around. More to see. Do you think they'll let me switch to the file room?"

"Hey," I said. "That's my job." I was trying to joke, but my tone was wrong, and it dragged across the smooth surface of the indifference I had spent weeks polishing.

"I'm not trying to take your job," she said. "I mean to take a few half days a week to help out in there. But I shouldn't ask you."

"You shouldn't," I said. "Ask Schiff."

"Not Mortenson?"

"I thought you were observing everything," I said. "Schiff will just say yes or no. With Mortenson, there's always a kind of dance." Telling her who had power was the only power I had.

Soon enough she had joined me in the file room two mornings a week. Schiff visited more than once each morning, and for a little while I was worried that I had miscalculated his interest in her. After all, behind his dolorous façade was a man, and a man would not have been immune to a girl like Lisa. But then his visits stopped, and it occurred to me that maybe his concern had been for me. I could see why. I knew things about the file room that she did not know, but she was a quick study, and by the third or fourth day she was correcting my errors or suggesting ways that work might be organized more efficiently. "A smart person wouldn't do this," she said, which made me dislike her a little and, predictably, want her even more. Lisa knew this and did her best to magnify matters. When we were having lunch, she directed her attention—both toward me and away from me, it is true, but she directed it. And I did what you do with direction: I followed it. "What are you doing?" she liked to say to me, no matter whether she had caught me looking or caught me not looking, and the tone was not coy or supportive but rather belligerent. I should have told her I was thinking of other girls, or even that I was thinking of her, or that her system for improving the file room was foolish, but instead I said too much by saying nothing at all. Days before, I had been certain that I wanted her but wouldn't act on it. Now I was less sure that I wanted her and less sure that I was capable of resisting. I had a clear line to my uncertainty and she was tangling it.

* * *

I HAD BEGUN TOYING with the idea that my future might involve, if not exactly writing, the management of written language toward some previously envisioned end, and in that spirit I started to ply Lisa with notes I left on her desk on the mornings when she did not join me in the file room. Most were officious in the extreme, which I intended as a form of modesty: "Ms. Foster," I'd write, "I hope you do not believe it has escaped my notice that you are filing your nails when you should be filing affidavits." Or, "I cannot express my disappointment strongly enough, so I will leave it to your evidently prodigious imagination, which you seem to be exercising rather than focusing on work." In the letters, I was authoritative, presumptuous, even rude.

One evening in the file room, I kissed her. I suppose it was predictable, but that did not make it any less miraculous for me. I credit, at least in part, her car. She drove a Toyota, brown with black vinyl, that baked hot in the afternoon sun, and she refused to leave the office until it had cooled off a bit. Since temperatures were routinely reaching ninety degrees, she was always there past seven, and just as I had gotten used to being the only one in the office late, I grew accustomed to being there late with her. We didn't always talk—it seemed too intimate—but sometimes I would drop by her desk to ask if she had received "Mr. Tipton's letter." One night, she came by the file room, even though she was supposed to be at the desk. She brought a transistor radio and a can of soda. "Care package," she said.

I did not answer. Or rather, as an answer, I slid my hand along the underside of her arm, closed my grip around her shoulder, and kissed her. She didn't return the kiss, not exactly, but she didn't pull away either. It was impossible to tell how she was feeling about the moment, and that was intoxicating to me. We kissed for a long time, and when I reached for the top button of her blouse, she pushed my hand away and unbuttoned it herself. Then she turned off the three long fluorescents that lit the room and backed herself against a wall in such a way that it seemed as though I were pushing her there. I waited for her to hike her skirt until I became aware that she was waiting for me.

Afterward, she excused herself and vanished downstairs to smoke a cigarette. I watched from the window as she puffed small clouds into the parking lot, looked back up to the eleventh floor, gave a wave of her fingers, got in her car, and drove off for home. No time had passed. I went back to filing.

The next morning, she was scheduled to join me in the file room, but she stayed at the beige cage to order office supplies. Once or twice I came out to ask her some minor question, and she answered with a nonchalance that was drenched in significance. She was mine, but not if I wanted her. And she was not mine in the way she had been a day earlier, when I had been secure in her friendship, desirous of more, and well aware of the importance of suppressing those desires. Now what was wanted clouded the air between us. I stayed in the file room, out of everyone's way, playing the radio a little bit louder than I knew was proper. In late morning, Schiff came into the file room, where he praised my efficiency and spoke to me for a few minutes about some new billing conventions that would affect the way we were accounting time on the Younce case but not the Jarney case. He did not dispense his usual aphoristic wisdom, and its absence was conspicuous. That, I gathered, was the day's lesson, that sometimes wisdom could abandon a man. I wondered how he knew about me and Lisa.

I wanted her to stay late that night with me. I thought I had

wanted things before, but I had been wrong; they were nothing in comparison to this. Instead, she asked me downstairs to
sit with her in her car while she smoked. She fidgeted nervously
with the lighter and left the cigarette unlit until I said what I
thought she wanted me to say, which is that the previous evening
had been a mistake, and that we needed to be friends above all,
because she was my only real ally at the firm, and that I wished
we could go back a day and undo what we had done. She agreed
too readily for my tastes, and patted me on the shoulder in a way
that precisely erased the kiss. With the situation now defused
and her power restored, she offered me a ride home, and though I
could have refused out of spite, or what I now can see would have
been power, I accepted with a shrug that could not conceal any
portion of my excitement.

The car was cooled off by now, and the whole way back we
carried on a polite conversation in washed-out colors. The next
morning, there were no longer even traces of that forced polite-
ness, just a humiliating normalcy. The subject had been dropped,
on account of its weight.

THE KISS HAD AN EFFECT on the rest of our friendship, as I knew
it would, but I could not have anticipated exactly what effect.
It was as if we had met for a meal and did not have much to say
about the food until a second spice was added, at which point
we realized that it had covered the flavor that we did not previously know had been there. That first flavor was on my tongue
constantly, and I was honor-bound to pretend it was not. She was
equally unwilling to admit that anything had occurred, and we
stood arm in arm on this dishonest foundation. Mortenson was
the first to notice, and he started to call us Ma and Pa. One after-

noon, he and Schiff called a meeting to settle up some business before they left the city on a trip. The agenda was brief—order supplies, schedule more interviews—but then Schiff said that he had an announcement. "We're going to give the two of you just one paycheck," he said. "We won't pay you less, but since you're always together, it's just easier that way." Lisa and I could have been offended, but we took it in stride. We were happily inseparable, bound as much by what wasn't happening as by what was. We were determined not to be dismissed as fools, and that determination was perhaps the most foolish thing of all.

Mortenson had said Ma and Pa, but there in the office, after hours, we were like the king and queen of the place. Sometimes I would stand at Schiff's window, and she would come up beside me and say, "Get to work." While I took calls from Schiff and Mortenson and ran into the file room to tell them which judge had presided over a certain case or what date a judgment was rendered, she spent an hour ordering lunch or performing what she called her "Goldilocks test," in which she sat in a series of chairs until she found the most comfortable. She called the local radio station and asked for her favorite songs to be played. The top drawer of the desk by the beige cage was filled with the Mr. Tipton letters, which carped about her lack of focus and drive; they were heaped in a pile to prove the point. Once, she went missing in the middle of the day; I patrolled the office until I found her in the stairwell, smoking a cigarette. She looked as though she had been crying. And more than once, when we were at work late, she took a glass out of Schiff's cabinet and filled it with whiskey. "To pleasure," she said, and then corrected herself. "To a few minutes of freedom." Her refusal to focus on work didn't bother me so long as she stayed late with me in our kingdom, but after that first week, she abdicated. She left earlier and earlier, sometimes even when the sun was still out. On those evenings, the office was dull: gray, flat, and silent.

But wonderful things happen in the dullest places. Sitting there in the conference room one night, knocking my foot against one of the legs of the table, I saw a comet streak across the sky. The janitor was the only other one there. He had just finished emptying the wastebaskets in the room. The air conditioner had started to power down for the night, and it was getting warm. I was trying to power down, as well, seeking what I would have described as peace, though I have realized as I have grown older that it is closer to humility. Just then, in the corner of the window, I saw what looked like a star moving.

I motioned to the janitor, asked him to verify what I was seeing. The comet moved more slowly, and it was larger to my eye than I would have expected. It passed behind a tree and reappeared. Now it was in the dead middle of the window, perfectly positioned to make a statement, and it flared brilliantly, like a piece of music, and vanished. "That was something," he said.

I went immediately to Schiff's office and dialed Lisa's number. This violated one of our unspoken rules, that when one of us was at home, the other did not intrude. "There was a shooting star, and it was huge," I said, throwing something extra into my tone to excuse myself. "It almost went all the way across the window."

"You're still at the office?"

I went for broke. "Yeah. I could come over."

"I don't think that's such a good idea."

"Well, then, you could stay late tomorrow."

"Good night, Jim," she said, but not unkindly, and she lowered the phone and then raised it again. "Ask me again one of these days," she said. Her tone gave enough away that I did not need to take the chance the next day, or the day after that. We kissed once in the stairwell, and once out by her car, and once when she was driving me home she stopped the car, got out, and let me press her up against the driver's side door. She said only my name, which almost made me forget myself.

SCHIFF AND MORTENSON HAD enjoyed some success with their trips and so they made more of them. That meant time for me and Lisa, but also an awareness that there was never enough time. They were always back too soon for my tastes, Mortenson in particular. He liked to look at Lisa, and though I could not blame him for that, I started to worry that he was looking not out of interest but with a professional eye. She was not, as I have said, working very hard, and a good manager could have put her right out of the office. That would have been worse for me than if I was fired directly.

Cases shifted and settled through June, and by the end of the month one in particular had moved to the front of the pack: the shooting in a motel complex in Georgia of a college football star. The young man, Lorenzo Francis, was staying at the motel with his girlfriend. When an off duty policeman who was also a motel guest saw what he thought was a drug transaction, he confronted the football player, who denied the accusation. After a scuffle, shots were fired, and Francis was hit by two bullets, one of which severed his spine and left him paralyzed. The officer remembered an attempted flight across a courtyard, but Schiff and Mortenson meant to show that the angle at which the bullet entered the body disproved this story, particularly with regard to location—in short, that he could not have been where he said he was when the shot was fired. To demonstrate this, they planned to use a model of the apartment complex.

This seemed like an opportunity for me to help myself. I went in to see Mortenson. "You need a model built?" I said.

"That's the word on the street," he said.

"You should ask Lisa," I said.

"Lisa?" He said the name as if he had not thought of her for days.

"Not to make it," I said, rushing forward. "I mean, maybe. But you should ask her because she takes architecture classes and I'm sure she knows people."

"That's a good idea," he said. When he turned, I saw a phone number on the paper. It was hers. He was already planning on calling. I did not even know if he was going to give me credit for the idea. I had parleyed and gained nothing.

Lisa went directly in to speak to Mortenson. I sat outside at her desk. I tried to see the office from her perspective, but it was difficult, since I could see her in the scene. Mortenson laughed and rubbed his bald head. She sat down and made her case: an architecture student would benefit the firm in this regard. A model was precisely what a student was trained to produce. She knew good people. Whatever they paid for the model, could they pay her as well for organizing it? There was something in her expression that was so strong it was almost a scent. Mortenson laughed again, and I had the sudden sense that it was all beyond me.

Mortenson buzzed the desk and asked me in. I entered the conference room and stood there wrapped in the sense that I had intruded. "There's one guy I think would be especially good," Lisa said. "His name is Jeff. I don't know him all that well, but he's the best model-builder in the class. He could do cutaway views, maybe even put some little lightbulbs in to show where the different people were. He has little kids and he's always talking about how he needs more money. I think he'd do it for cheap."

"Hi, there," Mortenson said to me. And to Lisa: "Lightbulbs. That's a great idea." And back to me: "Do you need her for something?"

"Something's wrong with the printer," I said.

"Okay," she said. "I'll be right there." She was quick to the door.

JEFF LELAND WORE HIGH-TOP SNEAKERS and a sweatshirt and his hair was held back in a ponytail. He sat so nervously that he should have stood: he jiggled his knee, fretted his wedding ring. I went to get him. "Hello," I said.

"Hi," he said. "Jeff. You must be Jim." I didn't like the way he said my name, or even his own. He was too easy by half, and that intimidated me. Now it seems comical, to have been intimidated by a man who was at most twenty-four or twenty-five.

"Follow me," I said. "Mr. Schiff and Mr. Mortenson are waiting."

I dropped Leland off. As I was leaving, Schiff called to me. "Stay," he said. I listened with professional interest, possibly for the first time in my life, as Schiff and Mortenson explained the case. The next day, when I told Lisa about the conversation, I found that I could replay a few notes but not reproduce the whole tune. Mortenson had drawn Jeff in by talking about his outfit. "Say that the cops see a guy dressed like you," he said, "and they assume he's up to no good. Is that just cause? And assume that this guy, the guy dressed like you, takes off at a clip, because he's afraid of what's going to happen to him, to his girlfriend. Do the cops call out to him? Do they order him to stop? Or do they just draw their weapons and fire at this guy who's like you?"

Schiff seemed disappointed that Mortenson would not bring himself to the facts. "But not *just* like him. Black. Let's not forget that. White officers."

"Right," Mortenson said. "Young guy. Black guy. Prime of his youth. Suddenly, his life as he knows it is over."

"He's not the jury," Schiff said.

"He might be," Mortenson said. "Or someone just like him."

"We just need you to make a model," Schiff said. "To show us how the apartment complex is laid out, to help us help a jury decide whether or not a man could have jumped from the landing to the middle of a stairwell without injuring himself."

"So what's the procedure?"

"Procedure's a grand way of saying it. We send you up there to that same motel. You stay there. You spend your time taking photographs and measuring, and then you make us a scale model of the place."

"How long will it take?"

Schiff paused judgmentally. "As long as you need for it to take." He turned to me. "Do you think he's up to the job?"

"He asked you that?" Lisa said as I told her the story.

"He did," I said.

"And what did you say?"

I was silent, just as I had been in the meeting. Lisa fell silent, too, and her face grew very serious, as a joke, and soon we were both too deep in the silence, and neither of us felt like smiling.

JEFF TOOK THE TRIP to make the model. Lisa called in sick while he was away. "I'm nervous," she said. "Maybe I gave them a bum steer." I told her she had nothing to worry about, secretly hoping I might be wrong. A week after Jeff returned, he brought in his model. He dropped it off, shaking hands with Schiff and Mortenson, and left without saying hello to either me or Lisa.

When I went into the conference room, Schiff and Mortenson

were standing next to the model. "Do you notice anything about this?" Mortenson said.

I did: it was beautiful, but it was not big enough to be seen clearly in court. "No," I said.

"Artists," Schiff said, "always prefer injustice to justice, whether they know it or not."

"He even put little handrails next to the stairwells," I said, trying to praise everything that was wrong about it.

Mortenson stood and came around the table. "The thing is, it proves our point." One of his fingers stabbed down into the courtyard. "There were echoes when the cop yelled. The sound bounced from place to place, repeating itself, but also erasing the first noise. There was no way for Francis to know where to look. He never had a chance." He shook his head with effort. "I'm sorry this kid screwed up the model. It may cost us a victory."

That night, Lisa agreed to drive me home. "I just don't understand," she said.

"What don't you understand? He botched it."

"There's no way to salvage it?" Her tone was pained. "I feel like I'm on the line." That night, trying hard not to help Jeff, I helped Lisa. I knew how to rescue the model, and came in early the next morning to explain the solution to Mortenson. He was instantly alive with the idea. "We put a camera right up against the model and give the jury a projection? This could work. This could work. Beautiful."

We took it to Schiff, who was in the conference room with the model. "I don't think it works," he said. "I think it's wrong to take to a jury."

"What do you mean?"

He wasn't the sort of man who was accustomed to explaining himself, but it was not for lack of skill. "It's just wrong. Putting a little camera in there and projecting the image on a screen would turn it into a show. The jury will feel it was made with a kind of pleasure, and that's the wrong message to send."

"I disagree," Mortenson said. "I think it's great."

"Do you talk so much so that you don't have to listen to me," Schiff said, "or to yourself?"

Ordinarily, Mortenson would have returned fire, and the volley would have gone on. But he just picked up the model and walked past Schiff silently. To ignore him outright was one of the most final things he could have done.

I WAS GLAD I HAD NO GRASP of the practical details of my plan, because it gave me a justification for involving Lisa again. She was good with those kinds of things, and she helped rig the camera and test the projection. The effect, the white model on the white screen, was both alienating and intimate. Mortenson was immensely pleased.

But Schiff was right. Schiff was always right. Whatever magic there had been in the idea—and in the office there had been a considerable amount—came off as legerdemain in the courtroom. I did not know this firsthand. I did not go to court. I could tell from the stormy look on Mortenson's face as he entered the office the day of the verdict. Schiff followed, triumphantly defeated. They had Stacy cut a check to Jeff and send it off and that was the last of him. Lisa began to work hard again in all things, convinced that she needed to prove her worth again. She also began to allow me more latitude in romantic matters, but it was the concession of a defeated woman. I accepted it nonetheless.

Over the next few weeks, Schiff and Mortenson grew apart. Lisa noticed first, and reported the breach in an aggrieved tone.

I nodded sadly. But perpetrators always think of victims: though Lisa had suggested Jeff, I had suggested Lisa, and when Jeff had failed the first time, I had rescued him so that he could fail a second time, more profoundly, and by doing so bring down the entire house. I knew that Lisa would figure this out soon enough, and that when she did, she would be gone.

It took a week. One Thursday night we were in her car, doing what we always did, when she announced that she felt something missing. "Is it your blouse?" I said. She laughed and drew close to me, but in drawing close she pulled away for good. She was giving me a farewell gift. The next evening, she left early. "I'm going out with friends," she said. "See you Monday." It put me in a black mood that permitted me to see everything else all the clearer, as a man in a darkened room at night has full vantage of the sky outside.

My situation, at any rate, was trivial compared to what happened to that little world I had inhabited. It had been teetering, I now saw, and before I could truly understand what that meant, it fell. Schiff and Mortenson were through with each other. It happened very quickly: one shouting match in the conference room in which the model was mentioned as proof of incompetence, withdrawn, and then thrust forward again with a stabbing motion. Mortenson stormed out and did not return, not the next day or the day after that. When he did, it was with a stack of papers that he said were for the purpose of dissolving the partnership. None of us could believe it, and we believed it less when they began to sign the documents. Schiff's signature on top, Mortenson's on the bottom: It was difficult to understand this togetherness in the service of separation.

Mortenson was the one who left, which was predictable. He was mobile. In fact, he could not stop moving, and the minute he was gone it seemed like a small miracle that he had ever been there at all. Schiff never regained his balance, morally speaking. After he parted ways with Mortenson, he became sullen and capricious. He would not come out of his house except to go to his office, and vice versa. Two weeks after Mortenson's departure, Lisa left to return to school. That was how my summer ended, and how the things in it ended, too. I went back to school. I graduated, aged, did my best not to let time do its worst to me. I wrote Lisa one long letter that I never mailed and eventually threw away, keeping only the envelope, which was addressed to her but not stamped. Years later, I drove by the building, checked the nameplate, relived that summer. Then I returned the car to the airport and flew back home.

ABOUT FOUR MONTHS AFTER my visit to Florida, I was traveling by train to my sister's home in Delaware, and as we pulled out of the Philadelphia station, I looked up and saw Lisa standing in the aisle. I had already experienced a sense of displacement, thanks to a young man I had seen when I was boarding the train. His hair was uneven to the left, as if put to the side by an idea, but other than that he was exactly what I was at that age. I put up my bag. I sat down, read a little bit of history, looked up, and Lisa was there.

We were in our fifties by then. Or rather, I should say that I saw with a start that she was, and I realized that I must be, too. I debated whether to reach out and tap her on the hip, and when I realized that the only thing deterring me was the idea that the gesture might be perceived as flirtatious, that was enough to push me forward. She turned and smiled even before she saw who it was. Then her smile vanished and returned, somewhat dimmed and thus more powerful. She sat down next to me. I tried to see her as she was, hopeful that it would help her see me as I was. Can a man be happy in memory or only lonely?

We had a grand old time, looking out the windows until night fell and making light of what we saw. After that we traded stories about the lives we had lived, and those we had failed to live. She had married a man who owned a small lumber company. The two of them had been through good years and bad years. They had two children who gave them equal parts joy and trouble. "I'm happy, but like everyone, I didn't do nearly what I wanted to do," she said. She did not, despite her story, look like a woman who had made sacrifices.

For my part, I told her that my first wife had been a poet, by which I meant an heiress, and that the union had ended badly, and that I had spent quite a bit of time living the bachelor's life before eventually finding a second wife. "No children," I said. "That's maybe the one abiding regret." We got, after a time, on to the matter of the office. I told her about my recent visit. "Same little building," I said. She asked me if I had heard that both Schiff and Mortenson had died. I said no but that I had assumed so. We sat in silence for a little while. She hummed, and I tried to recall her as a younger woman, when her papery skin was a pliant pink and the clothes she wore suggested their own absence.

"I remember that summer so well," she said. "Do you?"

"A little," I said, lying.

"Remember Jeff?" she said. I nodded. Now she was back in the past with me, or more accurately without me. "We had such a wonderful trip that week. I'm afraid I didn't let him work on the model even for a minute." She smiled at me. "You and I had quite a discussion about it, if I remember correctly."

We had not, of course, at least as far as I remembered. And I would have remembered. Still, it didn't surprise me; I may have suspected as much at the time, and by now I was far past being harmed even by confirmation. Still, and despite all the wisdom I believed I had acquired, I was overcome by a sense that all the time since had been miserably misspent, and that fear propelled me up from my seat.

"I could use something to wet my whistle," I said.

"Wet mine while you're there," she said, laughing. Her eyes went up coyly, as if she were a much younger woman.

I went off to the dining car. At the far end I noticed the young man I had seen boarding the train, the junior version of me. He was pushed up close to a young woman, speaking animatedly. "I don't know how you feel about me, exactly," he said. "You don't say."

"You're right," she said. "I don't say."

His head bowed in sadness. He was better than me at being me, right down to the failures.

I walked farther down the train, bought two small bottles of gin, and walked back up the train, and Lisa and I poured ourselves drinks and came back to the past. She had given me a story and so I gave her one in return. At forty I had thought I would remarry, but I lost the woman I loved—not to another man but to illness. At forty-five, I thought I would never remarry. At fifty, I met a woman in a downtown bar. I was with a man who fancied himself a poet. She was a dancer twenty years my junior, so beautiful she made me feel both too old and too young. I drank too much, as I always did in those days—"how else to ascend / the twin peaks of Truth and That Which Could Not Be Said?" as the poet had it—and I treated Mary, for that was her name, to a recitation that, I am ashamed to report, contained a rather lavish description of her physical charms. "It was as if my entire personality had its shirttails out," I said.

"And how did she respond?"

"She married me," I said. I put a twinkle in my eye.

"Wonderful," she said. "Just wonderful." She settled back into her seat. The train clacked along. I felt guilty for having lied. Or rather, for having told the truth without telling the whole truth. Mary was the kind of woman who was easily mortified. She had a distaste for confessionals, outsized announcements, and any other type of behavior in which decorum fell under the wheel. That day she had looked at me with dread and left the bar. She married me, but only after nine months of silence, and nine more months of begrudgingly cordial conversation. I was not restored to anything approaching amity until we had spent a chaste summer in the company of some friends on the Cape. Then came the romance, and the rigors, and the loss, and the retrenchment, and the courtship, and the comedy, and the declarations (mine) and the withdrawal (hers) and the reiteration of the declarations and the marriage.

I did not explain any of those things to Lisa. The past cannot learn from the present, no matter how much it aspires to. As we neared Delaware, I let the string of the conversation out to her. She was funny on the matter of her children, one of whom was adopted. She told me about vacationing out west when they were young and how the boys invented a game called "square-ball." I helped her stand when the train came into the station. Her arm was frail beneath my fingers. Time had taken its toll on the young bodies we remembered using for disreputable ends.

HER HAND

THE WOMAN INSPECTS HER HAND. SHE HOLDS IT AWAY FROM her face and looks at it as if it does not quite belong to her, as if its history is something she has read. Thirty-two years before, the hand had gone into her mouth regularly. Sixteen years before, it had unbuckled the belt of a young man who was watching television nervously in the basement of her parents' home. Eight years before, it had enveloped the tiny hand of her son as he put his lips around her nipple for the first time. Four years before, it had opened up the mailbox at her home, and everything had changed. The hand had survived the mailbox and the postcard it found there, the painful moments clutched in the other hand that followed closely behind, the jeweler's efforts to cut the ring off. It had been in flour and in water and in leather and in blood, in duress and in ecstasy. It had been in the garbage looking for a credit card that her son had accidentally thrown out. It had been between her own legs as a form of forgetting. Now things are back to normal, give or take. She withdraws the pile of mail, carries it to the kitchen table, brushes the cat with her other hand, sits down. She is looking for a letter from her son. It isn't the first thing off the pile, which is a flyer for singles cruises, or the second, which is a political circular. Third off the pile is a catalog for home furnishings; she considers going right past it, but she is charged with maintaining the household, and that is what you do when you maintain a household: you visualize possible improvements, rehearse the process of each item entering your house, try to imagine how it will affect the space. She's regretful by page three: there is an heirloom cherry sleigh bed that looks as though it belongs exclusively to winter. She feels certain she would wake one morning to find a reindeer curled on the floor beside her. There is a flat black dining table with green stone insets; it is majestic but would be too much at half the cost. On page nine she finds something she likes, despite its name: a "moon-shade wall/floor lamp," available in black or white. She rehearses the process of the lamp entering her house, tries to visualize it existing among the other elements. There is a word for this kind of exercise, the forward-cast of thought, but she can't remember it. She lifts her hand from the catalog and places it on her forehead. *Prolepsis*: that is the word. How would a moon-shade wall/floor lamp change the room? The couch would exhibit no reaction. The cat might turn away in chilly indifference. Her son would likely object; *horrendous* is his favorite word these days, and he finds plenty of opportunities to use it. Sometimes, when he calls home from camp, she tries to use the word back at him, to see if she can get him laughing at himself. But he is a great stone face on the telephone. His tone is flat and black. Her son has not always been this way. During the first four years of his life, he was a sweet boy, generous with his affection. She liked to watch him with his father, playing games of their own invention; she remembered telling people that it was nice to see a good father at work, and she remembered continuing to tell them that even after the good father declared that he was stepping down from the position. When her husband wasn't playing with his son, she remembered, he was usually complaining: about how life hadn't taken him far enough, about the shoddy work of others in his field. Once he wondered out loud if he would still be married in two years. Then, finally, engorged with his own doubt, he had retreated to a hotel in another city and announced that he was reconsidering the marriage. She was serious with him on the telephone, but as soon as she hung up she found herself laughing. She knew he had already decided as much as he was capable of deciding. Still, when the postcard came, she trembled, and when she finally worked up the courage to read it, she held it at arm's length as if to protect herself from the poison of the thing. After a few days, she told her son that his father was not coming home, at least not right away. She misrepresented his absence as a kind of vacation. When her husband did show up, it was only for a week, after which he moved out. He did several terrible things to her, mostly sins of omission, though his dedication as a father never waned, which filled her with a mix of gratitude and killing rage. She flips through the mail more rapidly. Bill, bill, bill. No letter from her son. Catalog, bill, magazine. Had the postal service slowed down? Magazine, political advertisement, bill. The letter has to be there, but it isn't. Her hand pushes away the mail; she goes to the couch, lies down, switches off the small red lamp on the side table, and forgets. She gets up, makes herself a snack, and goes back to the mail with renewed resolve. She shakes out every magazine in search of the letter and finds nothing. Finally it falls out of a lingerie catalog. But it isn't a letter. It's a postcard. She kneels, trembling, and inspects it. The handwriting is like her husband's, but it's her son's. It has to be, and so it is. She picks up the postcard and reads it. Her son is writing about a new friend he has found, and how thrilled he is to be at camp, and how he wants to visit the friend over the winter, and how he is sorry that he acted so churlishly the first few weeks of camp. Churlishly? she thinks. She stares at the back of the postcard and tries to visualize her son writing the word. Then her hand sets the post-card down on the flat white surface of the kitchen table, locates a letter-opener, and starts to slit the bills open, one by one.

ACKNOWLEDGMENTS

Acknowledgments always give me cottonmouth. How can you possibly measure who contributes to a book of short stories? Some people were models for characters, with consent. Others were models for characters, less consensually. Some people provided support. Other people provided competition. Others still sat near me in an airport or a restaurant, just for a minute, but had a look about them that got me thinking. There are hundreds of unknown collaborators and co-conspirators who cannot be named and of those who can be named, I will expose only a fraction of them. Thanks to Cal Morgan, for editing and publishing me. Thanks to Ira Silverberg and Ruth Curry, for representing me. Thanks to Gail, for marrying and tolerating me. Thanks to Daniel and Jake, for being top-drawer kids. Thanks to Lauren, for being a top-drawer friend. Thanks to my parents, Richard and Bernadine, and to my brothers, Aaron and Josh. And thanks, finally, to the novelists, short story writers, songwriters, and filmmakers whose work I depend upon every day of my life for . . . well, for life. By making things, they make the world and have helped me come a long way from unaware.

Insights,
Interviews
& More . . .

Meet Ben Greenman

Dorothy Hong

WHEN I WAS IN COLLEGE, I had a habit of walking out of parties minutes after walking into them. The reason was simple: I didn't like the sadness. I'd come into the room, and it was like I was walking into a sliding glass door of shame, embarrassment, and self-hatred—and not just my own. I'm not saying people didn't have fun at parties. People had fun. But the fun was created, to some degree, by the sadness. It was the negative space carved out of the unfun. I didn't like it, and when it started creeping up my spine, I left. Later on I learned some strategies for blocking out the sadness I was absorbing from the room, most of which involved poor eye contact and a steady stream of jokes. We do what we can with the tools we have.

After college, I followed the vertices of a triangle: I went back to Miami, where I had grown up, to work as a newspaper reporter; went back to Chicago, where I was born, to attend graduate school; then went to New York, where I became a magazine editor and started to publish books of fiction. Recently, while I was on tour for

> 66 It was like I was walking into a sliding glass door of shame, embarrassment, and self-hatred— and not just my own. 99

my last book, *Please Step Back*, I found myself once again in O'Hare Airport in Chicago, where I sat and watched the people pass by, their brows furrowed with one worry or another: maybe the mortgage was late or the insurance on the second car was too expensive or the husband was putting on weight in a way that seemed to indicate depression or the stepson was developing violent tendencies or the boss wasn't showing enough respect or the lover wasn't loving back the way she used to or the mother needed surgery. I had forgotten what I had known in college, but now I remembered it suddenly. Every expression, every gesture, seemed to broadcast sadness. I put my earphones in to block it all out and went to get something to eat.

As I sat and ate my sandwich, I saw a woman sitting by herself, also eating. It was an airport. People eat alone all the time. There was no reason to make too much of it. And yet, the more I watched her, the more I was sure that she was sad, and not sad in a transitional or instrumental way, but deeply, foundationally, irreversibly sad. She was in her mid-thirties, attractive but tired-looking, reading a business report filled with black-and-white charts. At one point, she took out her cell phone, started to make a call, and thought better of it. The hand holding the phone sank down until it was in her lap. I had taken my earphones out. I put them back in.

A few days after that, I mentioned the woman in the airport to a friend of mine, and she was silent for a long time, which was her way of letting me know she was angry. My problem, she finally said, wasn't that I was mistaken in assuming ▶

that these other people's lives were sad—she agreed that they were, for the most part—but that I acted as though they were different from me. "Well," I said. I didn't know what I was going to say after that. Luckily, she went on. She said it made her angry that I wouldn't just acknowledge their sadness and that I felt compelled to push forward with a kind of dumb combination of empathy and superiority. "Well," I said again. She had to go, she said. She went.

I thought about what she had said, and for a few minutes it seemed true. But then parts of it started to shimmer, like a mirage, and I wasn't as certain anymore. The part about connecting to the common humanity in us all had a certain appeal, but the part about rejecting the temptation of that dumb mix of empathy and superiority bothered me. Isn't that where much art comes from? You feel the pain, it starts to drive you to your knees, you bring yourself back up by telling yourself you don't belong down in the pain, you move forward on this cushion of temporary superiority, and then you use the energy generated by this process to create something. In fact, after a few times, you come to value the sadness, to receive it with a kind of joy, because you know that it will, in time, bring you to creative work.

This principle, with some important variation, has been at the center of most of what I've written: collections (*Superbad*, *A Circle Is a Balloon and Compass Both*), novels (*Superworse*, *Please Step Back*), short stories, humor pieces, and essays. I write often about sadness and loneliness, which are present in all of us but which are harder to detect (if easier to feel) amid the modern-day rush of communications technology. The only cure, I think, is intimacy, which is what the people in my stories are struggling to achieve. Many of the stories in this book are set in the past, recent or distant, before the Internet and Facebook and Twitter began frittering away at legitimate human connection, and as a result the characters are preoccupied with conversation and correspondence, with voices and faces.

A while back, I wrote a story called "Snapshot," which was about a middle-aged Russian researcher, a widower, and his epistolary friendship with an American scientist. The Russian does not know that the American is a woman until she sends a newspaper clipping that includes a photograph of her, at which point the Russian does what a man should always do when he encounters a woman who intrigues him—he studies the evidence:

He mounts the photograph on the wall over his workbench. As the afternoon proceeds, he comes to understand it better. Some of the heaviness of her face results from the shadow cast by the figure to her left, a well-known Harvard mathematician whose name he cannot recall now. And while the woman is older than he initially suspected—at least forty, he now guesses—he can see her twentieth year in the playful tilt of her head, her tenth in the unguarded brilliance of her smile. But it is her eyes that draw him most powerfully, with such a luminosity that looking into them, even through the intervening medium of the photograph, is like listening to the voice of their owner.

It's probably narcissistic, and certainly solipsistic, to try to prove a broader point about mankind by quoting from my own work, but that paragraph goes to the heart of the sadness I assume is in most human interaction, even (especially?) when it is in pursuit of happiness. Another friend of mine, who is a young adult writer—I mean that she writes for young adults, not that she herself is a teenager—once told me that I was good at "funny sad you know," which I initially took as an insult but came to wear as a badge. I learned to wear it as a badge because I shined it up and saw what she meant. By "you know," she didn't mean to be dismissive, but rather to isolate a certain dedication in my work to expressing both what is funny and what is sad—and, at the same time, to acknowledging the limits of expression. I have a third friend who once asked me why I write mostly about human relationships. "There's more," she said. She's wrong. There's not more, or at least not a more important job for fiction. You can (and should) stretch that theme around whatever frame you want, and put whatever frame you want around that theme. Stories can take place, as they do in this collection, in the distant past in wartime, in the recent past on the moon, on the imaginary border between two noncontiguous countries. No matter where they're set, and no matter when, they explore the way men and women delight and infuriate each other, and in doing so illuminate my sense that this is still, after all these centuries, humanity's proper central preoccupation. ▶

Meet Ben Greenman (*continued*)

I have recently started a few new projects. I won't say too much about them, because I'm superstitious, but they have to do with some or all of the following topics: shaving, sweatshops, safety inspection, magicians, evolutionary biology, squids, football, the Great Mosque of Damascus. In every case, though, those topics are masks that fit over the faces beneath, and the faces beneath are the faces of men and women, trying their best to seek out the most satisfying companionship and fellowship. Scientists can make science meaningful. Clergymen can make God meaningful. Architects can make space meaningful. Musicians can make sound meaningful. I can only try to make language make life meaningful, and only for a little while. Funny sad you know: we do what we can with the tools we have. ◟

" I can only try to make language make life meaningful, and only for a little while. "

A Conversation
with Ben Greenman

Ben Greenman is the author of What He's Poised to Do, *which was first published in 2008 as a limited-edition boxed set called* Correspondences.

Alex Rose is a writer and designer and the publisher of Hotel St. George Press, which published Correspondences.

Cal Morgan is Ben's editor and the editorial director of Harper Perennial. They discussed the project in a midtown Greek restaurant in October 2009.

CAL: Let's start at the beginning. Ben, what inspired these stories in the first place?

BEN: For years, I've been writing about what happens between men and women. In earlier collections of mine, like *Superbad*, my interest in those themes might not have been as apparent, because the treatment was more experimental and often heavily comic. It was with *A Circle Is a Balloon and Compass Both*, in 2007, that I began to explore them more deliberately. I wondered: We have put people on the moon. We have split the atom. So why have we made so little progress in understanding how men and women deal with each other: the want, the wait, the hope, the hurt, and so forth?

CAL: And did you know from the start that you wanted to use letters to tell these stories?

BEN: Well, all words are made of letters.

CAL: Hilarious. I mean the other kind of letters: the ones people write to each ▶

other. The first version of this collection was published in a limited-edition box called *Correspondences*. Was it designed explicitly as a set of stories about letters and letter-writing?

BEN: I started from the idea that I was writing stories about the disconnections between people—about romantic frustration, about misunderstanding. And then I noticed that many of them were set in the recent past, at a time when people communicated (or miscommunicated) through letters. That's where Alex came in.

CAL: Alex, you run an innovative, small publishing house in Brooklyn called Hotel St. George Press. How did you connect with Ben for this project?

ALEX: I had always been a fan of Ben's writing, as far back as *Superbad*, and I met him at a party in Brooklyn. I was talking to Ben's wife, Gail, not knowing she was married to him, and I happened to mention that I dug Ben Greenman. She said, "That's my husband. Hey, Ben, come meet a fan!" I thought she was kidding, but there he was. We immediately started talking about doing a book together. At that time, Aaron Petrovich and I had done a few titles with Hotel St. George, but we were looking to shift from trade paperback to handmade letterpress books. We wanted to work more directly with our authors, to go beyond just taking a manuscript and putting it between covers. We wanted layout and typography to reflect or amplify the themes of the book.

BEN: This would have been at the beginning of 2008. I had a novel, *Please Step Back*, coming out in 2009. I didn't want to shoehorn in another traditional book in the midst of that schedule, but the idea of doing a nontraditional book really appealed to me.

ALEX: Right. We pretty quickly realized that the running theme of letters was a way to unite these stories into a collection, but then we had to decide what "collection" meant. These were also great stories about human interaction, thwarted love affairs, rivalries, disappointments, and enduring love, and I noticed that there were invisible threads that connected the stories.

CAL: What do you mean by invisible threads?

BEN: Yeah. What do you mean?

ALEX: I just thought that sounded cool. No: themes would recur, as in any collection, but in interesting ways. There was the story about a man who came from Cuba to the United States and continued to write letters to the woman he loved there, even after she was out of his life; to me, that seemed connected to another story, about a guy in Nebraska who was grappling with a troubled marriage. When Ben came up with the idea that these weren't connections, but correspondences, that gave us an organizing principle and a title: *Correspondences*.

BEN: It probably started as a pun, but then it turned into something much richer—thanks in large part to the design. Alex and Aaron designed a box with four foldout panels; each panel held a little accordion book, and each little accordion book contained two stories. Those were the pairs of stories that I saw as corresponding with each other, just as the characters in the stories advanced their lives by corresponding with each other. And then we came up with the Postcard Project to complete the package.

CAL: Tell us more about that.

ALEX: When we designed the case, it was meant to hold eight stories in four accordion books. Then one afternoon we started talking about the fact that the box was a very exclusive form. It folded up. There was a bellyband around it. It kept people out, in some way. As a remedy, Ben suggested writing a story that was intentionally incomplete and inviting readers to contribute to it. We printed that story, "What He's Poised to Do," on the actual casing, and then we put a postcard in the fourth pocket, where the fourth booklet would have gone. The reader got to write back to us, the publisher, to complete the story. We posted some of the responses to the Mail Room of the Hotel St. George Web site.

BEN: People loved that Postcard Project.

ALEX: I think it brought in a different kind of appreciation. Because the box was a high-end, limited-edition object, I thought we'd get attention from design magazines and book blogs. We did. But then there were all the people who seized on the idea of the Postcard Project as an interactive fiction experiment. Which was cool, but also a little frightening. When something sounds "high concept," ▶

A Conversation with Ben Greenman *(continued)*

people sometimes assume it's not superior to a description of itself—that it doesn't transcend its own novelty.

CAL: Funny you should say that, because that's how I encountered it. I was out in Los Angeles on business with Carrie Kania, our publisher, and we went into Book Soup, the wonderful bookstore on Sunset, and both of us were exploring the store, looking for hidden treasures. At one moment or another, each of us separately stumbled across an elaborate endcap display the store had devoted to *Correspondences*. I was astonished by the innovative approach to the form and the intricacy of the package. But I didn't buy it then, in part because I was worried about crushing it in my luggage, but also because I was feeling protective of it. I knew Carrie would love it the way I did—this is the kind of thing we're always driving each other crazy with—but I felt such a sense of discovery, and I wanted to be able to order it when we got back and present it to her as if out of nowhere. Back in New York, I walked into Carrie's office, and there was a copy on her desk. She'd bought it at Book Soup and hadn't mentioned it to me.

BEN: It's like an O. Henry story.

CAL: It gets stranger. A few months later, I was judging a live fiction event in New York for *The L Magazine*, and Ben and Aaron Petrovich were two of the other judges. We were all introduced, but it was only after we'd been there a while that I realized that these were two of the people responsible for *Correspondences*: the author and the publisher. At that point, I hadn't yet read beyond the cover story: I think I was so taken with the box as an object that I was reluctant to read further into the collection. Then I went home and read the stories, and they were exquisite. I was entranced by the elegance of Ben's writing, and by the fact that his characters were flesh-and-blood people, even the ones he found odd. I called Aaron, and we started talking about developing a more traditional paperback edition.

ALEX: Did you think right away that you'd need to add stories?

CAL: I thought it would be important, yes. Luckily, Ben had written more.

BEN: I wrote more pieces as a direct result of that original box. I did lots of interviews about the HSG edition, and often the interviewers' questions actually sparked new stories. In the spring and summer of

2009, I went on tour for *Please Step Back*, and that strange journey—cities I didn't know very well, people I met on the road—also helped with new material.

CAL: My sense of Ben's vision for this new version came into focus after he sent me his first version of the full collection; a number of the added stories were longer, more complex pieces that extended what he'd done in the earlier stories.

BEN: In a strange way, the second phase worked like a correspondence between me and the original box.

ALEX: I notice that you decided to keep "What He's Poised to Do," which was the interactive story connected to the Postcard Project.

BEN: We did keep it, after some discussion.

CAL: It might be an understatement to say we kept it. It became the title story.

BEN: But it's no longer interactive. For this edition, we decided to do without the participatory element of the story and let it stand on its own, as a kind of establishing vignette.

CAL: For me, that story was always the keystone of the collection. So many of the ideas that define your stories—alienation and intimacy, communication and miscommunication, honesty and dishonesty—are traced in those few pages.

ALEX: Ben, do you think of this new collection as an extension of the original edition? As an evolution?

BEN: I'd say it's a complement. There's overlap in the stories, of course, but there are enough differences, in both content and design, that they feel like separate things.

CAL: Though there was one bit of continuity that was important to us when we offered to take the project over, which was to ask Hotel St. George to design our edition as well. We loved the original box so much, and felt that it had such power, that we wanted to bring at least some of that into the traditional book form.

ALEX: I thought it would be interesting to have a subtle design element that reminded people that these are stories about (and ▶

A Conversation with Ben Greenman *(continued)*

around) letters, as well as stories that span the globe, and so I came up with this postmark idea.

BEN: I'd say that the book-box, *Correspondences*, has its own pleasures, and that the book that's not a box, *What He's Poised to Do*, has its own. In terms of the stories themselves, this version feels a touch less tricky in conception and execution, a touch more straightforward.

CAL: But there are still a few little tricks throughout.

ALEX: Like what?

CAL: Like the way the stories interact with each other. They don't all correspond in exactly the way they did in the box, but there are tiny echoes throughout. In "A Bunch of Blips," a woman gets involved with a series of men, and one of those men seems to be a character from another story. The woman in "Her Hand" might be the woman who's married to the man in "What He's Poised to Do," but later. Blood in one story seems to flow into another story. A bird from one story might fly into another one.

BEN: Some of those echoes are intentional, and some are just possible, as you say. I'm always suspicious when the characters in a story collection seem to have *nothing* to do with one another: to me, that seems artificial. At the same time, I didn't want to link them together too mechanically. I just wanted the stories all to take place in the same universe, and to address the same set of concerns: men, women, love, lust, loss, comedy, tragedy, pleasure, pain, and lunar settlement. So that little tissue that connects all the stories is a fictional version of the real-life tissue that connects us. ∽

Further Explorations

If you've just read *What He's Poised to Do*
and enjoyed it, you might enjoy the
following as well. If you haven't, but
you've enjoyed any of the following,
you might enjoy *What He's Poised to Do.*

Søren Kierkegaard, *Either/Or* (1843).
The philosopher Kierkegaard's work is
often used to cudgel undergraduates into
submission, which is a shame, because he's
also one of the most playful and inventive
writers of his or any time. *Either/Or* is one
of the best examples of how to build an
argument using multiple perspectives,
layered narrative, fragmentation, and
pseudonymity.

**Henry James, *The Princess Casamassima*
(1886).** James is the author I return to
more than any other, in part because I'm
constantly trying to untangle him—at the
level of sentences, at the level of thought—
and in part because I find the books
immensely pleasurable. No one has done
a better job at observing the way light plays
on the surface of human consciousness.
This novel is considered something of
an oddity for James because it deals with
politics more explicitly than most of his
work, but for me that helps bring the vexed
inner life of its protagonist, Hyacinth
Robinson, into sharper relief.

**Duke Ellington, *The Blanton-Webster
Band* (1940–1942).** There are three names
in the title: the composer and pianist Duke
Ellington, a leviathan of American jazz,
and two members of his band of the
early forties, the bassist Jimmy Blanton ▶

and the tenor saxophonist Ben Webster. The title leaves out so many more who made this music, including the arranger Billy Strayhorn, the alto saxophonist Johnny Hodges, and more. But you'll find them soon enough when you immerse yourself in this music, which ranges from near-novelty up-tempo songs to the saddest dirges.

Groucho Marx, *You Bet Your Life* (1950). Groucho was long past his prime as a vaudevillian and movie star when he agreed to host this not-very-interesting game show. What made it good, and then great, was his willingness to engage with the contestants, to lead them into genuine conversation and/or put them at the spear-end of his wit. Groucho to young actress: "Now suppose you became a famous actress, and then you met somebody you liked and got married. Would you be willing to quit acting and be a housewife and a mother?" Young actress to Groucho: "Well, I think if you keep your feet on the ground you can combine both. That's what I'd like to do." Groucho to actress: "Well, if you keep your feet on the ground, you'll never be a mother."

Charles Laughton, *The Night of the Hunter* (1955). The great actor Charles Laughton directed only one movie, this Southern Gothic tale of crime, punishment, innocence, and (especially) evil. Robert Mitchum personifies the last, as a preacher who roams around the countryside marrying vulnerable women and then snuffing them out. Shelley Winters is also superb as one of those women. But the real star is the direction—particularly the art direction, which results in several moments that are almost Goya-like in the way they combine terror and profound morality.

Stanley Elkin, *The Dick Gibson Show* (1971). Elkin struggled with multiple sclerosis for most of his adult life, yet regardless of how his illness limited his physical energy, he was one hell of a dervish on the page, turning out a series of genuinely unhinged but impeccably written comic epics. *The Dick Gibson Show* follows the picaresque adventures of a radio host in the broad midcentury of America. William Gass has said that Elkin was like a jazz player, and William Gass should know.

Swamp Dogg, *Cuffed, Collared & Tagged* (1972). There are very few genuine moralists/ironists in soul and funk music. Swamp Dogg is one. He's been doing it for forty years, and he's not done yet. The fact that he recorded a song for my novel *Please Step Back* isn't a factor in my recommending him without reservations. People like to point to the first Swamp Dogg record, *Total Destruction to Your Mind*. I like to point to this one, which has his peerless cover of John Prine's "Sam Stone" and a great tribute to Sly Stone, without pointing away from the other.

Joy Williams, *State of Grace* (1973). The world can be a terrifying place where certainties wither and die and what's left behind are either husks or seeds. This ▶

novel, by Joy Williams, goes straight into the middle of the strangeness of people—particularly her conflicted, half-lidded heroine—and it's one of the most poetic books of the last half century.

Mary Margaret O'Hara, *Miss America* **(1988).** There are eccentrics in pop music, and then there are Eccentrics: artists who put every last bit of their elusive, misshapen, but still beautiful personality into their work. Mary Margaret O'Hara's one of the archetypal Eccentrics, and her sole solo album, *Miss America*, is one of the strangest pop records that also makes perfect sense.

Paul Beatty, *Joker Joker Deuce* **(1994).** I read lots of poetry, but I don't understand it. Or rather: I love watching words play, but not all of them are my kids. Or rather: I like it when I see someone walking around, shining like a high-watt bulb, phrases and fragments spilling out of his pockets. Or rather: Sooner or later, someone was going to fuse the verbal energy of hip-hop with the formal rigor of poetry with the confusion of modern life. ∾

Don't miss the next book by your favorite author. Sign up now for AuthorTracker by visiting www.AuthorTracker.com.